ACKNOWLEDGMENTS

With many thanks to the dauntless filmmakers and the erudite publishers, who have shown me amity and candor from the moment I started this project.

I am so grateful to Toni Atterbury and her assistant, Lauren Widor. Special thanks to Nancy Kirkpatrick, Amanda Boury, Andrea Johnson, Gillian Bohrer, Larissa Saenz, and Derek Schulte at Summit. A big thanks to unit photographer Jaap Buitendijk and to all of the folks at Industry Art Works, including Andrew Hreha, Andrea Miner, Denise Balbier, and Ashley Barb.

It was a joy to meet so many members of the cast and crew on set in Chicago, including Neil Burger, Doug Wick, Lucy Fisher, Alwin Küchler, Andy Nicholson, Jim Berney, Carlo Poggioli, Greg Baxter, Brad Wilder, Denise Paulson, Shailene Woodley, Theo James, Ashley Judd, Maggie Q, Tony Goldwyn, Ray Stevenson, Ben Lloyd-Hughes, Christian Madsen, Amy Newbold, Mekhi Phifer, Miles Teller, and Ansel Elgort.

This book would not have been possible without Jill Davis at Katherine Tegen Books at HarperCollins or without Katherine Tegen herself, who brought me into her family of authors. Molly O'Neill, also, was welcoming and wonderful. Laurel Symonds was a great support. I would also like to thank designer Victor Ochoa, as well as Barbara Fitzsimmons, Rick Farley, Joe Merkel, Melinda Weigel, Gwen Morton, Josh Weiss, and Shayna Ramos.

And finally, of course, this book belongs in spirit to the prodigiously talented Veronica Roth. I'm in awe of your imagination and your gifts!

"MY NAME IS TRIS."

DIVERGENT

OFFICIAL ILLUSTRATED MOVIE COMPANION

BY KATE EGAN

KT KATHERINE TEGEN BOOKS
An Imprint of HarperCollins Publishers

Jaap Buitendijk, who photographed the filming of *Divergent*.

Katherine Tegen Books is an imprint of HarperCollins Publishers.

Divergent Official Illustrated Movie Companion
™ and © 2014 Summit Entertainment, LLC;
text copyright © 2014 by Veronica Roth. All rights reserved.

Photos on pages 10, 20, and 32 courtesy of Veronica Roth;
page 11 (top) © 2011 HarperCollins Publishers;
page 27 courtesy of Joanna Volpe;
page 30 (top) courtesy of Becky Anderson;
page 30 (bottom) French jacket art © 2011 by Editions Nathan Jeunesse;
page 31 (top) Brazilian jacket art © 2011 by Editora Rocco, Ltda.;
page 31 (top) Spanish jacket art © 2011 by RBA Libros, S.A.;
page 31 (top) Russian jacket art © 2011 by Eksmo Publishers LLC;
page 31 (top) Italian jacket art © 2011 by Istituto Geografico De Agostini;
page 40 (bottom) © 2011 by Merie Wallace, courtesy of Fox Searchlight Pictures;
pages 41 (bottom) and 44 © 2013 by Wilford Harewood, courtesy of A24 Films;
page 52 licensed by Warner Bros. Entertainment. All rights reserved.

Library of Congress Control Number: 2013956488
ISBN 978-0-06-231562-5

Book design by Victor Joseph Ochoa
14 15 16 17 18   LP/RRDRK   10 9 8 7 6 5 4 3 2 1
❖
First Edition

CONTENTS

THE STORY OF *DIVERGENT*   8

MOVING TOWARD A FILM   22

A SEARCH FOR THE PERFECT CAST   38

TRAINING   58

BUILDING THE WORLD OF *DIVERGENT*   64

A LOOK FOR EACH FACTION: 100
COSTUMES AND MAKEUP

SHOOTING THE FILM   124

THE STORY OF
DIVERGENT

Above: Author Veronica Roth.

Bottom right: Shailene Woodley as Beatrice "Tris" Prior.

FORCED TO CHOOSE...

In a future world that's neatly divided into five factions—Abnegation (the selfless), Amity (the peaceful), Candor (the honest), Erudite (the learned), and Dauntless (the brave)—you'd think it would be easy to find your place. After all, each faction embodies one of the best qualities in human nature. And within any faction, a person finds community. Responsibility. Love. It's a simple but satisfying system.

Unless you don't fit in.

Sixteen-year-old Beatrice Prior, born into Abnegation, knows she doesn't belong fully in any of these groups. Her aptitude test has revealed something terrible: She's suited for more than one faction.

Divergent, it's called. In this world, that's a dangerous thing to be. Peace and stability depend on people pledging loyalty to one faction above all else—even family. But a person who doesn't fit into any category could have divided loyalties. And a person with divided loyalties might not be easily controlled.

Beatrice can't share this secret with anyone, not even her parents. But now she knows there's a reason she's never felt quite like the rest of her quiet, self-sacrificing family. Now she knows why she's always been drawn to the daring Dauntless kids at school. She could be one of them, too, if she wanted.

Tomorrow, she will have to choose.

The faction system allows Beatrice to leave Abnegation for another faction at the Choosing Ceremony. There's only one catch: It will mean cutting ties with her family forever.

Poised at the edge of adulthood, this girl must make a permanent and life-altering decision, with consequences she can't foresee. Should she stay safe inside the limits she has always known, together with her family? Or should she take a chance on what's in her heart and leave everything else behind?

Veronica Roth sets up this conflict in the opening chapters of her stunning 2011 debut novel, *Divergent*. It's as if she has distilled the entire teen experience into these few pages, recognizing that moving into adulthood can also mean leaving beloved people and places behind.

As Roth explains it, "I think it's the classic coming-of-age moment, but exaggerated. At some point in your life you have to decide if you're going to stick with the way you were raised and fully commit to what your parents have taught you to do, or to listen to your own internal compass. And sometimes your internal compass leads you to where your parents actually wanted you to go. I don't think any teenager's really experiencing this on quite so intense a level, but I think it's the reason so many people have connected to the story."

What will Beatrice choose? The rest of Roth's ambitious tale unfolds from this question.

When Beatrice chooses to go—and to grow— she leaps into Dauntless, a faction that's the opposite of everything she's known before. In Dauntless, she accepts challenges and embraces dangers that leave her both terrified and exhilarated. She grows close to other

> ## "I THINK IT'S THE CLASSIC COMING-OF-AGE MOMENT, BUT EXAGGERATED."
> —Author Veronica Roth

people for the first time—including Four, the mysterious instructor with whom she has an electric connection. She becomes, in some ways, the person she's always wanted to be. She even gives herself a new name: short, sharp Tris.

Tris is uniquely unqualified for the rigors of the Dauntless initiation, which require her to be aggressive in a way that would never be allowed in Abnegation. If she fails, though, Tris will be factionless. Homeless, abandoned, and alone. Somehow, she finds the strength to push through.

But *Divergent* is much more than the story of a girl beginning to shape her own destiny. Roth also uses her novel to explore the limits of a rigid utopian society. The aptitude test and the Choosing Ceremony exclude and deny Divergents. But it's in her Divergence, finally, that Tris finds her greatest strength. When she embraces the full range of her qualities as a human being, she can play an active role in her world. Even as it is falling apart.

While once Tris believed that the factions lived side by side in peace, she understands her world differently now that she's inside Dauntless. There's tension among the initiates from different factions, and that tension reflects what is happening beyond the Dauntless pit. Erudite is moving against Abnegation to seize control of the government. Then the Erudite will use the Dauntless—the society's soldiers—to do their will.

Left: The Prior family hugs before the Choosing Ceremony (L to R: Ansel Elgort, Tony Goldwyn, Ashley Judd, Shailene Woodley).

Above: Still called Beatrice (Shailene Woodley), she makes her decision at the Choosing Ceremony.

"YOU'RE NEVER GOING TO WIN. NOT LIKE THAT."
—Four (Theo James)

Left: Tris (Shailene Woodley) and Four (Theo James) on the Ferris wheel during Capture the Flag.

Right: Tris (Shailene Woodley) prepares to jump into the Dauntless compound.

But there are some Dauntless who can't be controlled. The ones who are Divergent . . . like Tris.

Against the twin backdrops of a crumbling utopia and a powerful first love, Tris must forge her new identity, accept what it means to be Divergent, and find a way to protect the family she's left behind.

Author Veronica Roth did not set out, at first, to write a dystopian novel at all. When she was in her first year of college, she began with a single image of a person jumping off a building, as a test of bravery, and started to ask herself some questions. Who would do that? she wondered. And why?

In the psychology class she was taking at the time, Roth remembers, she was studying exposure therapy. "It's a way of treating people with anxiety and phobias in which they are repeatedly exposed to the stimulus that frightens them," she says. "So someone who is afraid of heights will go into an elevator for longer and longer periods, say, until their brain rewires and they're not as afraid of that thing anymore." When she thought of the person jumping off the building, she saw someone trying to face their darkest fears.

Soon she invented the idea that this person—a boy she was calling Tobias—would confront his fears in an artificial environment, sometime in the future. "So the idea for Dauntless came from these simulated environments in which a person can encounter their fears safely," Roth recalls. "And the theory of the Dauntless is that over time the fear will be gone and you'll create fearless people."

If there was a group where people tried to conquer fear, Roth decided, there could also be other groups in her futuristic setting, each dedicated to conquering other flaws in the human character. If all the groups succeeded, they'd have a society that lived together in harmony and peace.

"THE IDEA FOR DAUNTLESS CAME FROM THESE SIMULATED ENVIRONMENTS IN WHICH A PERSON CAN ENCOUNTER THEIR FEARS SAFELY."
—AUTHOR VERONICA ROTH

Roth says, "The other factions evolved when I thought, 'If I were creating a utopia based on eradicating personality flaws, or fostering virtues, which ones would I choose? Which ones would be most important?' So after Dauntless came Abnegation, because I think that selfishness is a pretty easy explanation for world problems. And Erudite, or intelligence, came after that. Then Amity—peaceful friendship—and Candor, because it occurred to me that honesty would also be important.

"But the trick with this," she continues, "was finding out that, even though this is my utopian vision, something about it is flawed. This is all supposed to be good for society, right? But

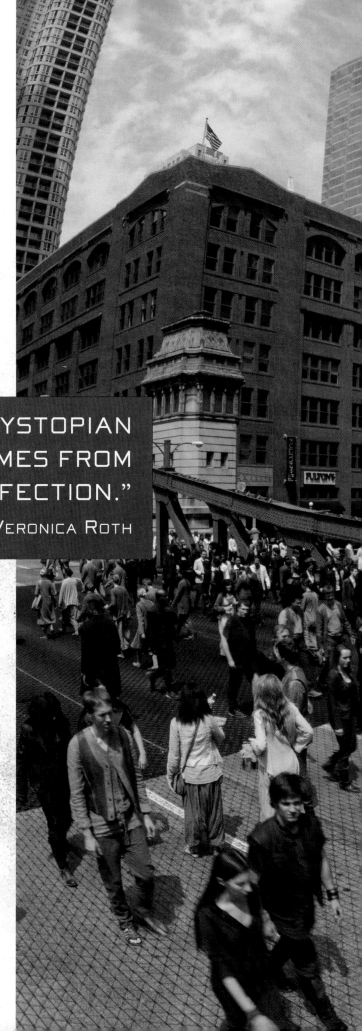

> ## "IT'S A HALLMARK OF DYSTOPIAN FICTION THAT IT COMES FROM SOMEONE'S VISION OF PERFECTION."
> —AUTHOR VERONICA ROTH

really, it's not. I had to figure out how the virtues would go wrong." Taken to extremes, she knew, even the best human qualities would go sour. Roth explains, "It's a hallmark of dystopian fiction that it comes from someone's vision of perfection." While the factions start with a commitment to certain ideals, the ideals erode as they meet the realities of daily life.

With her ideas for the Dauntless and the other factions, Roth began to write Tobias's story, but she got only about thirty pages in before she realized it wasn't working. For several years, then, she put the story aside.

Cast members from all of the factions mill about in an opening scene of *Divergent*.

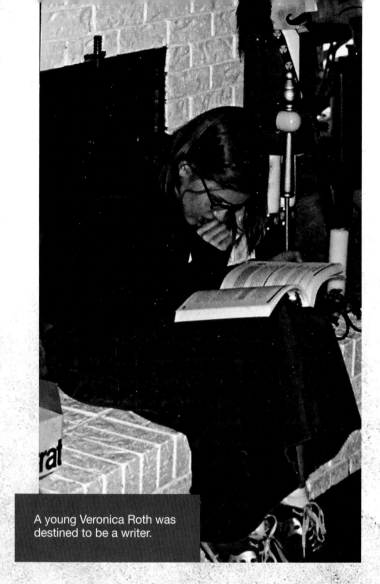

A young Veronica Roth was destined to be a writer.

"I'm not really sure why it didn't work with Four as the protagonist," says Roth. "I think part of it is that it's a little more interesting to tell the story of a young woman leaving a perfectly safe, very controlled environment, and going into an incredibly dangerous and risky one. There is something, given our cultural climate, that makes that a more interesting story. We might expect an impetuous young man to join Dauntless, so that wouldn't be surprising to us. But a young woman choosing Dauntless—especially a very small young woman—this is crazy! So maybe that's why the story ultimately worked when I chose Tris as the narrator."

After she imagined Tris, Roth's disparate ideas suddenly came together into a compelling whole. Roth remembers, "I was pulled in by Tris. I was fascinated by her voice, and I first wanted to create the circumstances in which that voice emerged, and then see what she could tell me about what was happening in her world." Undistracted by schoolwork, Roth focused on this project over winter break, and it rapidly grew to the length of a novel.

Fast-forward to Roth's senior year at Northwestern University, where she was studying creative writing. She had always loved science fiction and fantasy, as well as young adult novels, including *The Giver* and *Ender's Game*. For her coursework, though, she was writing nothing of the sort. Few of the other students shared her interest in these genres, and her assignments required a different kind of voice. Roth still worked on her pet projects, during late nights or over vacations, but she didn't share them with her classmates.

That year, Roth decided the story about Tobias needed an overhaul. Tobias would remain a character, but the story would be told from a different point of view, that of a strong and unyielding Abnegation girl named Tris.

Then, in storybook fashion, things changed very dramatically for Veronica Roth. Some months before this, she had attended a writers' conference, connected with a literary agent— Joanna Volpe—and submitted a manuscript to her, which Volpe ultimately rejected. When the story of Tris and Four was finished, though, Roth sent it to Volpe first. Within one month, Volpe agreed to represent Roth and also sold the rights for the entire Divergent trilogy (which was not written yet) to Katherine Tegen Books, an imprint of HarperCollins Publishers.

Not bad for an author who was about to graduate from college.

Arriving at the height of a red-hot moment for dystopian young adult fiction, and offering just the right balance of full-throttle action and powerful romance, the book was a sensation before it was even published. Buzz built within the publishing company as editors Molly O'Neill and Katherine Tegen shared the manuscript with their marketing and sales teams. Booksellers and librarians devoured the advance copies, certain they were reading the next big thing. Roth stoked the excitement as well, with her candid and approachable blog. When the book was finally published in May 2011, it debuted at number six on the *New York Times* Best Sellers list and kept climbing steadily to the top spot.

By then, a film was already in the works.

Right: Author Veronica Roth's first visit to her publisher's headquarters in New York City.

Below: *Divergent*'s debut on the *New York Times* Best Sellers list.

6	**DIVERGENT,** by Veronica Roth. (Katherine Tegen/HarperCollins, $17.99.) A girl must prove her mettle in a dystopia split into five factions. (Ages 14 and up)	1
7	**A WORLD WITHOUT HEROES,** by Brandon Mull. (Aladdin, $19.99.) A young boy is transported to a world ruled by an evil wizard. (Ages 8 to 12)	8
8	**HOORAY FOR AMANDA AND HER ALLIGATOR!,** written and illustrated by Mo Willems. (Balzer & Bray/HarperCollins, $17.99.) Stories about a surprising friendship. (Ages 4 to 8)	2
9	**THE EMERALD ATLAS,** by John Stephens. (Knopf, $17.99.) Three siblings discover a mysterious book that unlocks a powerful prophecy. (Ages 8 to 12)	5
10	**ABANDON,** by Meg Cabot. (Point, $17.99.) A supernatural romance inspired by the myth of Persephone. (Ages 12 and up)	2

MOVING TOWARD A FILM

Author Veronica Roth with producers Doug Wick and Lucy Fisher.

ENTER HOLLYWOOD

Red **Wagon Entertainment** producers Doug Wick and Lucy Fisher came upon the manuscript before it was published and were smitten with what they read. They immediately brought the book to Gillian Bohrer, Executive Vice President of Production and Development at Lionsgate. Gillian remembers reading *Divergent* for the first time one weekend in January 2011. As the book wasn't published yet, she was reading photocopied pages in a coffee shop, and the page that described Tris's decision at the Choosing Ceremony was . . . missing. "I had to know what happened!" says Bohrer. "I read ahead and

figured it out. And then I couldn't stop reading. I just couldn't put it down."

That Monday morning, she started spreading the word at Summit. "I knew the story would break through to a movie audience," Bohrer remembers. "It had so many themes that would resonate with teens, from challenging your limits to finding your own family. Plus it had these amazing set pieces, from the Choosing Ceremony to the Ferris wheel and the zip lining. . . . I could see them in my head, just when I was reading, and I knew they would make for a fantastic film."

When Summit's Erik Feig was in New York a few weeks later, he met with Veronica Roth's film rights manager, Pouya Shahbazian. "Erik Feig came in with a game plan," Shahbazian says. "A playbook. He loved the novel, and Summit knew to a T what it would take to make *Divergent* into a larger franchise." Two months before the novel was published and became an immediate success, Shahbazian and Red Wagon sold the movie rights to Summit, with partners Red Wagon attached to produce. "Veronica's books are so well written and the characters are so engaging," says Rob Friedman, cochairman of Lionsgate Motion Picture Group, "that readers become captivated from the very first page. As a studio, it is stories and the characters found in book series like Divergent, which make for great source material for film. When you have great content, it becomes easier to bring it to life. We are fortunate that Veronica chose Summit Entertainment to be a partner to create a visual experience that matches what she has worked tirelessly to create. We look forward to delivering what we collectively have worked on with the release of *Divergent* and can't wait to see subsequent films based on the franchise."

Summit Entertainment was the studio behind the wildly successful *Twilight* films as well as *The Hurt Locker*, the 2010 Academy Award winner for Best Picture. It had a proven track record of making high-quality films as well as lush adaptations of young adult properties. And the Red Wagon producers, Doug Wick and Lucy Fisher, had been in the business for decades, creating classic films from *Gladiator* to *The Great Gatsby*.

Unquestionably, Roth and *Divergent* were in good hands.

"VERONICA'S BOOKS ARE SO WELL WRITTEN AND THE CHARACTERS ARE SO ENGAGING."
—ROB FRIEDMAN, COCHAIRMAN OF LIONSGATE MOTION PICTURE GROUP

Author Veronica Roth with producer Lucy Fisher.

Doug Wick also remembers reading the book for the first time and being struck by its epic reach. Of the many potential projects he was considering at the time, *Divergent* stood out right away. He explains, "For me, it always starts with the story. And *Divergent* takes elements of a whole lifetime and compresses them into one moment in Tris's life. These are universal themes: You leave home, and your parents become a sort of blank to you. Then you begin to realize that they're more than you thought they were. At the same time, you move from familial love to romantic love. Later, you integrate romantic and familial love. And then you lose your parents . . . so much of this arc appears in *Divergent*, and we're only with Tris for a few months of her life."

Wick felt an immediate connection to the story and saw many opportunities to make a film version of *Divergent* that was narratively and visually stunning. *Divergent* could deliver action and suspense, but at its core would be a character very different from the kind of character you'd usually find in an action film. Like Veronica Roth, Wick was captivated by Tris's strength and determination. "With a female protagonist, we'd breathe new life into a genre," he says. "Male clichés have become tiresome in action films. But credible, strong female protagonists . . . that was a huge untapped opportunity."

In addition, he loved that the novel gave readers unique access to Tris's inner life in the fear simulations, and he was eager to take on the challenge of dramatizing them on film. In these sequences, filmmakers would be able to access Tris's thoughts and feelings in a way that movies normally don't allow.

Above: Tris (Shailene Woodley) and Four (Theo James) explore Four's fear landscape.

FINDING A SCREENWRITER

Producers Wick and Fisher, in cooperation with the team at Summit, began to explore how they would translate Roth's story into a different medium. The first step would be to develop a screenplay; from that, everything else would follow. Summit and the producers asked screenwriter Evan Daugherty, who had recently written *Snow White and the Huntsman*, to adapt Roth's novel.

Daugherty remembers what initially drew him to the project: "Tris starts off in this incredibly sheltered, selfless, peaceful world, and then basically she decides to join the equivalent of the navy SEALs. That's a big character arc—it's fun to track that," he told bloggers at Bookish. Daugherty responded viscerally to the book's action sequences, but in the screenplay he took great care to balance them with the growing romance between Tris and Four. "It's important that the chemistry between them doesn't just feel like it's thrown in," he explained, "but that it helps Tris grow as a character." Skillfully, he showed Tris's character development within the framework

of fast-paced action and ensured that each fear simulation scene drove the story forward.

When the screenplay was complete, and all involved were pleased with it, the search for a director began.

Above: Author Veronica Roth with screenwriter Evan Daugherty.

Below: A page from the *Divergent* movie script, nicknamed *Catbird*.

CATBIRD   Goldenrod - 04.25.13   96.

           FOUR
Requisitions for war. Sent by
Erudite.   *
                                                  *

           TRIS
     (realizing, horrified)   *
They're going to war with
Abnegation.   *

           FOUR
Not them.
     (showing her)
Us.

           TRIS
Us? Why would *we* fight for
Erudite? We wouldn't.

           FOUR

...WHO WILL DIRECT?

Summit and the producers had a long list of qualities they'd be looking for in a director. He or she would need to have great visual style and be able to elicit strong performances from young actors. They needed to feel up to the challenge of making an epic movie set in the future. They needed to be able to show the characters' inner lives through the simulation sequences. And they needed to have great instincts as a writer and a storyteller. Who could possibly meet all of these criteria? One of the first names that came to mind was that of director Neil Burger.

Lionsgate's Gillian Bohrer remembers, "The fear sim sequences would be like playing in a sandbox—any director would love the opportunities they offered. But we knew that Neil [Burger] would do more than make them visually striking. He would make audiences feel they were with Tris every step of the way."

The director of a wide range of movies, from *Interview with the Assassin* to *The Illusionist* and *Limitless*—as well as a writer himself—Neil Burger was already aware of *Divergent*, and not sure he was eager to make a science fiction film. His feelings changed completely once he read the screenplay. "I liked that the script didn't have creatures, or sci-fi artificial things in it, or superheroes," recalls Burger. "And I loved that it was set in the future, but not about futurism. Instead, it uses a futuristic world to explore human nature. The script asks universal questions about loyalty. Tris asks 'Who am I loyal to? Myself? My family? Or my faction?' These questions are not unique to young adults, which I like. And *Divergent* shows a very different kind of future than we've seen in other movies."

Neil Burger directs Shailene Woodley (Tris) and Amy Newbold (Molly).

"HE WOULD MAKE AUDIENCES FEEL THEY WERE WITH TRIS EVERY STEP OF THE WAY."

—GILLIAN BOHRER,
EXECUTIVE VP OF PRODUCTION &
DEVELOPMENT, LIONSGATE

A VISION FOR *DIVERGENT*

A group of enthusiastic readers with Veronica Roth (center) at Anderson's Bookshop in Chicago.

Burger, Summit, and Red Wagon all shared a vision for the film version of *Divergent*. Even though it was set in the future, they all wanted the movie to feel current and relevant, as if it was really about *now*.

Once Burger signed on to direct—and began assembling a team that included a director of photography, a production designer, a location manager, a costume designer, and so forth—the whole group needed to articulate what that vision would really mean. Where would they make the movie? What would it look like? Who would the actors be? Preparing to shoot the film would take much longer than the shoot itself, as the team would plan every scene to the smallest detail.

The story would be told through dialogue, of course, rather than the narration of the novel. Screenwriter Evan Daugherty had already condensed a nearly 500-page novel into the

130-page script that would serve as Burger's road map. But before Burger could get to the work of directing actors in performing that script, he would need to find ways to expand and extend all the visual detail that Roth had described in her book.

Above: French editions of *Divergent* and *Insurgent*.

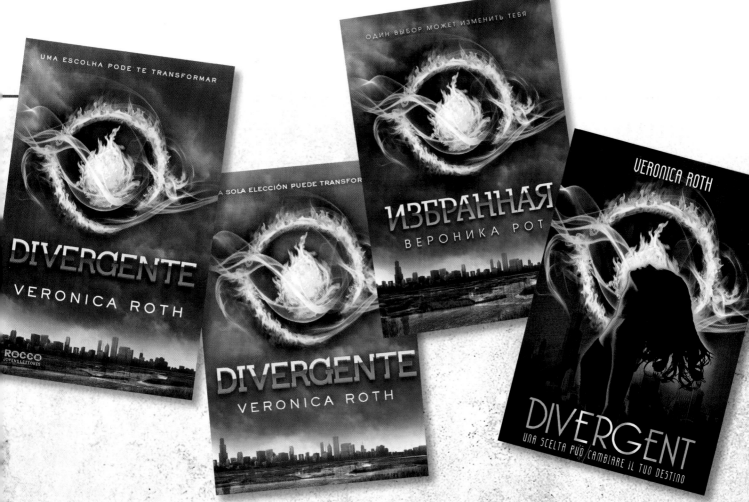

Early on, soon after the film rights were sold, Roth had met with producer Wick. At that point, she was less than a year out of college and on the verge of a kind of success that most people her age could only imagine. Roth remembers, "I wasn't sure what to expect, but he was just so nice and so concerned about other areas of my life, like what it felt like to have this happen when I was only twenty-two. It felt like he was concerned about me as a human being, and that went a long way toward making me feel comfortable handing over my work to be interpreted by someone else."

When the time came to expand on what she had written, then, Roth "had a little conversation with myself about ownership. When I write the story and it's just in my computer, I'm the one who owns it. I control everything about it. But then when the book gets released, it suddenly belongs to millions of other people who are reading it. So that transfer of ownership happens from the second other people start reading the book. And it's the same with the movie. The story now belongs not just to me, not just to the readers, but also to the director and to every actor they cast."

Top: Four of the thirty foreign editions of *Divergent*: (L to R) Brazil, Spain, Russia, and Italy.

Above: On the *Divergent* set with author Veronica Roth and producers Lucy Fisher and Doug Wick.

Author Veronica Roth is crushed by her editor's notes on the massive *Allegiant* manuscript.

THE DETAILS EMERGE

By the time Burger consulted Roth about some of the details, Roth was well into writing *Allegiant*, the third book in the Divergent trilogy. She knew how Tris's story would turn out, and she also knew more about what had happened, long ago, to create her dystopian society in the first place. Roth spoke at length with Burger about this backstory and shared information that no one but her editors knew yet. "I spoke with Neil about the surrounding world, and what had led to the city being created. He needed to know if he should depict any kind of destruction, and where it should be, and why it was there. I think Neil probably knows the most secrets of anyone," Roth says. Still, Burger was curious about details she had never even considered.

She continues, "Neil asked me a lot of 'detail' questions, ones that Tris was unlikely to answer in the narrative—how does commerce work in each faction? Do the factions ever work together? What does that look like? Would there be any Amity present on Visiting Day? What kind of physical destruction is present in the city? Like that. In a movie, more so than in a book, you can show the world of a story in brief but significant ways— a shot of people walking down the street, for example, can contain a wealth of information. Neil wanted to make sure that the world surrounding the narrative made sense, that there weren't any inconsistencies in the world-building, and that the world was rich. I'm not a big 'describer,' so seeing someone take my sparse settings and make them beautiful and detailed was . . . inspiring. Incredible."

With Roth's help, Neil Burger came to a basic understanding of the kind of society he would be showing on film. It would be about 150 years in the future, but a hundred years after an event that caused all technological advances to stop. Burger and his production team would need to imagine fifty years from now, and then decide what might be left over a century after that. What kinds of structures could withstand that test of time? What could be created from the few remaining raw materials the people had? None of these details were spelled out in Roth's novel, but the filmmakers would use them as background as they began to make decisions about design.

The story is set in Chicago, a city of millions of people, but in Roth's future city there are only about thirty thousand people. "They're occupying this grand, slightly abandoned place," says director Burger. "They keep up the areas that they use, but then there's a vast area of the city which is kind of crumbling and falling apart. When we see the city, we just see people walking in the middle of the streets, because they don't have cars. There are a few trucks around, but mostly their transportation is on foot or on train." He and Roth even discussed what people in this city might use for power. If they had it, how did they get it? Eventually,

he came to the idea that there could be wind turbines on the sides of some buildings and power cables swooping between them.

Roth smiles when she remembers some of her discussions with the filmmakers. "When I wrote the book, I was mostly concerned with Tris's internal life, and she doesn't notice all the details. She's not a big describer of settings so, you know, I wasn't thinking about what the chairs looked like or the needles looked like. I would never have been able to imagine all of that. Neil Burger has been one of the most detail-oriented and thoughtful people I have met through this whole experience. Talking to him, I'm sometimes like 'I wish you had been here while I was building this world, because I think it would have been a little more fully realized if you had been around.' He's just so concerned with every little piece of the society and with representing it properly, even in the background."

On location in Chicago, author Veronica Roth talks with director Neil Burger.

A CITY BECOMES A STAGE

As his vision of this future Chicago began to come together, Burger came to an important conclusion: The real Chicago would be the only place to make this movie. Veronica Roth, in fact, had come to a similar conclusion as she was writing. "In the rough draft, the story wasn't set in a real place—the world of *Divergent* was just a nameless urban environment," she recalls. "And when I revised it, I realized that I wanted a greater sense of place to make the story feel more real. When I was trying to figure out the real environment it could take place in, I looked at what I already had, and I realized I had already set it in Chicago without meaning to, probably because it's the city that I know and love the best."

Just as Roth knew her story would resonate with readers if it were set in a recognizable place, Burger felt that the best way to make his film seem relevant and relatable was to plant it someplace real. Once he'd made up his mind, he didn't even consider other possibilities.

Making a movie in Chicago would create certain complications: Transportation could be difficult in a major city at rush hour, for instance, and renting urban space could strain his budget. But with a real city as his stage, Neil Burger knew he could create a certain look. He remembers, "Even though it's set a hundred and fifty years in the future, we're on the streets in the real sunlight against the real buildings, and that just gives the film a completely different kind of energy than we see in other films set in the future. I knew I wanted to use Chicago as Chicago and shoot scenes like street photography, almost. I wanted it to look fresh and unusual."

To create this effect, Burger sent location manager James McAllister on a mission to identify as many Chicago locations as he could. Before the rest of the film crew arrived, McAllister was visiting every notable spot in town.

And at the same time, Burger was beginning to assemble a cast.

Left: At Chicago's Navy Pier: the Ferris wheel, as imagined concept art in the film.

Below: Chicago's famous skyline.

"I HAD ALREADY SET IT IN CHICAGO WITHOUT MEANING TO, PROBABLY BECAUSE IT'S THE CITY THAT I KNOW AND LOVE THE BEST."
—AUTHOR VERONICA ROTH

Concept art for Chicago of the future, including the El train tracks.

A SEARCH FOR THE
PERFECT CAST

WHO WILL PLAY TRIS?

Divergent **would feature** an ensemble of young actors, training and growing together. At the same time, though, Burger's group would need to find an outstanding group of adult actors to anchor the young cast. With the proper combination of new and familiar faces, the film would appeal to as wide an audience as possible.

Doug Wick's philosophy on casting was this: "The actors we cast are like magnets at important moments in the story. Four had to have a powerful pull or the story wouldn't work. We have to have actors who can deliver meaningful performances at these critical moments." Across the board, then, director Neil Burger's team would be looking for actors of the highest caliber.

The first priority, they decided, was to find their Tris. Shailene Woodley, of Simi Valley, California, was an up-and-coming actress with critical acclaim for her performance in the 2011 film *The Descendants* and starring role in the television series *The Secret Life of the American Teenager.* She was filming another

novel-to-screen adaptation, *The Spectacular Now*, when Burger's team approached her for the part. Woodley had the right look for Tris, as well as the wide range that an actress would need for the part. What they didn't know was that Woodley was also a down-to-earth young woman who would be more than able to handle the action and stunts involved in the role.

> # "THE ACTORS WE CAST ARE LIKE MAGNETS AT IMPORTANT MOMENTS IN THE STORY."
> —PRODUCER DOUG WICK

Producer Lucy Fisher says, "I think it was probably the easiest bit of casting that we ever did. We thought we were going to have a long search, meet every cool young actress. Then we met Shailene and it was like . . . game over. Obviously we loved her in *The Descendants*. But she also likes to go and get dropped off in Maine for two weeks, then live on her own with a hatchet and a few other things. Her Dauntless side was just hanging out there."

Woodley could see the dramatic possibilities for the character at once. On one hand, she found Tris's situation terrifying. Woodley says, "Once you leave the nest in the *Divergent* world, there is no going back. And that's incredibly frightening. I can't imagine never speaking to my mom again because I decided to go travel the world, or go off to college."

At the same time, though, she understood the appeal of Dauntless for Tris. Woodley continues, "To wonder what it would be like to do something, and never do it . . . I can't imagine doing that, and Tris doesn't want to be that person either. She can't imagine staying in one place to please someone else, and

that means she's not really selfless enough to stay with her family. Also, joining Dauntless is an adventure. She has a new freedom she couldn't picture in her previous life, and that's very exciting to her."

Veronica Roth embraced Woodley as the movie Tris. She explains, "Tris is kind of a complicated character. She's not always very nice—she's like an impetuous teenager. She's not always so mature or developed in her thinking. So I think Shailene's kind of gotten all the shades of Tris, and it feels very real every time that she says something or does something. It's like a revelation, a whole new way of seeing this person that I created."

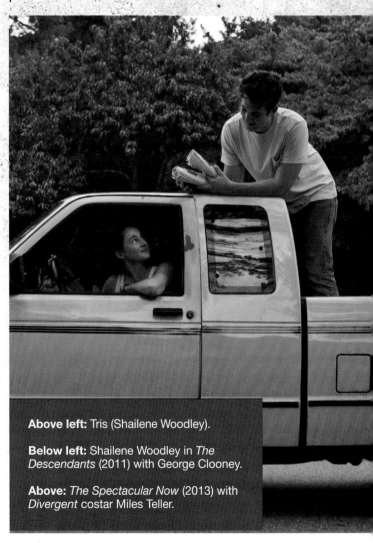

Above left: Tris (Shailene Woodley).

Below left: Shailene Woodley in *The Descendants* (2011) with George Clooney.

Above: *The Spectacular Now* (2013) with *Divergent* costar Miles Teller.

LOOKING FOR FOUR

Finding Woodley's costar, the actor who would play Four, was not as simple. Neil Burger and the producers auditioned dozens of actors for the part, testing them with Woodley, but none of them seemed quite right for Four. Lucy Fisher remembers, "The search for Four was like one of those old-fashioned movie searches that you hear about in the 1940s, where you sort of go to every country, you look at everybody. We knew this part would be complicated, because Four had to be manly and rugged, yet he also had to be soulful, and he had to be a good match for Shailene Woodley, who is a tough girl."

Casting offices in five cities around the world were busy looking for the right actor, and Lionsgate's Gillian Bohrer estimates that they considered almost four hundred actors for the part. "We needed to find someone that you'd believe had been through a lot before this story began," she explains. "We needed to find someone who was a physical fit for Shailene Woodley, who is quite tall. And we needed to find someone who could convincingly dominate her, at least at the beginning, but it seemed like most of the guys were following her lead."

As they tested for Four, the team discovered many other actors they liked for different parts, and several of them came to form the core of the Dauntless faction. Miles Teller, for instance, had just finished filming *The Spectacular Now* with Woodley, a film in which their characters fell in love. In *Divergent*, though, he was cast as Dauntless initiate Peter, one of her greatest foes.

Shailene Woodley as Aimee and Miles Teller as Sutter in *The Spectacular Now*.

This was a very different kind of movie from the last one the pair had made together. "In this world there are no boundaries," says Teller. "Men fight women and vice versa. So there were some things I had to sort of justify in my own head before we started." With Neil Burger's help, he came to realize that Peter would feel threatened by Tris. "Anyone who might be ahead of Peter—jeopardizing his staying in Dauntless and fulfilling his dream—that's a problem," says Teller. That explained why Peter was able to fight so viciously, and why he was so eager to turn one of Tris's friends, Al, against her.

Actor Christian Madsen, son of actor Michael Madsen, was just getting his career off the ground. As he was in the process of moving out of his apartment—because he couldn't pay the rent—he got a call from his agent. He wasn't cast as Four, but he'd been offered the role of Al, the transfer from Candor. Before the news even sank in, Madsen was calling his landlord to ask for a second chance.

Madsen related to Al's quiet, watchful character, and even his physical size. "Al is an interesting case," says Madsen. "He's very shy—a searcher—and he takes this leap of faith to join this faction." Once he's in Dauntless, he can see the many ways it will be hard for him to fit in—until Tris reaches out. "Tris helps him to open up," explains Madsen. "She says hey, you're a big guy—use that. You're very shy out here—don't be that way. She kind of shows him who he can become." Madsen imagined that Al was pressured by his parents to take on a new identity, while Tris encourages him to accept himself as he is.

Top: Miles Teller (Peter) and Shailene Woodley (Tris).

Bottom: A scene between Tris (Shailene Woodley) and Al (Christian Madsen).

Neil Burger directs Ben Lloyd-Hughes, who plays Will.

British actor Ben Lloyd-Hughes was cast as Will, a transfer from Erudite who becomes one of Tris's good friends. He was drawn to the idea of Will as a truly strong character who makes choices for principled reasons. "Anyone who changes faction in this world is a rebel," says Lloyd-Hughes. "So there is a part of Will that's a rebel. But there's also a part of him that's drawn to this idea that he can be brave. That he can make the noble decision and the honorable decision and stand out from the crowd in the best possible way."

"ONE OF THE THINGS THAT RESONATED WITH ME WAS THAT IT FELT LIMITLESS. THERE WASN'T JUST ONE STORY TO BE TOLD . . . AND THAT WAS VERY INTERESTING TO ME."

—MEKHI PHIFER (MAX)

Mekhi Phifer, who plays Dauntless leader Max, remembers reading the script for the very first time. He says, "One of the things that resonated with me was that it felt limitless. There wasn't just one story to be told. There are multifaceted characters and issues that could be brought to light, and that was very interesting to me." In addition, he liked the idea of being part of a film project that his family would want to see. Even though Max is the leader, Phifer points out, it is actually Eric—his deputy—who's the darker character.

Right: Max (Mekhi Phifer).

Below: Eric (Jai Courtney).

While Eric seems to lack any feeling for the initiates, the actor who plays him, Jai Courtney, dug deep to understand Eric's inner life. "I didn't want him to be this villain in the background who's kind of twisting his mustache and plotting," Courtney says. "It needed to be about more than that for me. As an actor, no matter how nasty your character is or what they're capable of, you have to find compassion for them. In some ways, I guess, I play the drill sergeant role in the training process. But Eric, my character, is also tied up with this super-objective, to take things over eventually, so he's got an ulterior motive."

As Christina, Zoë Kravitz—the daughter of Lenny Kravitz and Lisa Bonet, and star of *X-Men: First Class*—immediately clicked with Woodley. Like their characters, the actors became fast friends. Kravitz explains, "Christina's relationship to Tris is like mine with Shai in real life. They meet early on, and they've both transferred. They've both just left the factions of their birth to join Dauntless. And they both just have this immediate connection, like you do when you meet someone on the first day of school. They're both really honest and brave and a little scared at the same time."

Woodley and Kravitz were joined by Amy Newbold, a newcomer, as Molly. A Chicago native, Newbold had recently left her job as a casting director's assistant to become a nursing student, but the casting director called her when she saw that *Divergent* was looking for an actor with Newbold's body type and coloring. The character she read for, Molly, was defined by her physicality, and Newbold had only ever taken a couple of kickboxing classes. She nailed her first read, though, and went right into training with the rest of the Dauntless crew. Of Newbold, producer Lucy Fisher says, "It's really fun to have somebody who has not worked before turn out to be such a star."

From left to right: Molly (Amy Newbold), Christina (Zoë Kravitz), and Caleb Prior (Ansel Elgort).

New Yorker Ansel Elgort would play a role that was set apart from the other actors. While most of them were members of the Dauntless pack, Elgort took on the role of Caleb, Tris's brother, who leaves Abnegation for Erudite. Elgort was intrigued by the character. "He really chooses faction over blood," Elgort explains, referring to a phrase that echoes throughout the film. "He truly thinks that Erudite is the faction that should be in charge. Since he's coming from Abnegation, his mind is empty, ready to be corrupted, so he believes a lot of what he hears when he transfers." Elgort's character has a long journey ahead of him, in *Divergent* and its sequel.

> "HE TRULY THINKS THAT ERUDITE IS THE FACTION THAT SHOULD BE IN CHARGE. SINCE HE'S COMING FROM ABNEGATION, HIS MIND IS EMPTY, READY TO BE CORRUPTED."
> —ANSEL ELGORT (CALEB PRIOR)

As the training continued, the final roles of *Divergent* were cast. As producer Doug Wick tells it, "Part of Tris's becoming a powerful person is facing off with someone even more powerful than she is. The stronger her antagonist, the more profound her rite of passage." He knew they would want a famous actor to play Jeanine, the dangerous leader of Erudite, but even he was surprised when producer Lucy Fisher decided to pursue Kate Winslet—star of *Titanic* and the youngest actress ever to receive six Academy Award nominations. Wick says, "Lucy knew we had to find someone big to play Jeanine. That's why she went after Kate Winslet. Kate is associated with quality and taste—and here she's the antagonist, which is a departure for her.

As soon as you have an actor with her stature on board, your project has new credibility within the creative community."

Veronica Roth could hardly believe what she was hearing. "They kept telling me who they were approaching for the adults' roles, and they said they were going to talk to Kate Winslet, and I was like, ah, good luck," she says. "I'm like a defensive pessimist. I just don't believe that anything is going to work out until it does. So when Ashley Judd and Tony Goldwyn and Kate Winslet were cast, I just didn't know what to do with myself anymore! I just wrote a series of exclamation points on my Tumblr and my Twitter, because it was all I could say."

The role of Jeanine was unlike any Kate Winslet had tackled before. "She's a master manipulator," Winslet explains. "And it's been fascinating for me to play someone who is quite blatantly cunning and manipulative, because it's not really in my nature at all. I've never really played an evil person before now. So it's been amazing to try and get inside the mind of a person like that. Taking over the world is pretty much her goal. She's a very clever piece of work."

Although the film is based on a young adult novel, the veteran actors all knew they were signing on for a movie for adults as well. For instance, Tony Goldwyn (of television's *Scandal*) related to the script both as a son and as a father. "I think Veronica Roth has hit on something so classic, in terms of a rite of passage," he explains. "Every one of us needs to claim an identity for ourselves and figure out who we are, even while it means differentiating ourselves from our parents. It can create tremendous anxiety and uncertainty, even trauma."

But if it is traumatic for the person making the choice, it is also traumatic for the person left to deal with the consequences—in this case his character, Tris's father, Andrew Prior. Goldwyn says, "Andrew's tragedy is of losing a child, but he's not just feeling the personal loss. He is aware of how the world is changing and frustrated that Tris doesn't understand the impact of what she is doing. Andrew knows that Jeanine will use Tris's defection against the faction. But he's dealing with a daughter who just doesn't get it. In an Abnegation-type way, he tries to make her understand what the consequences of her behavior might be."

Above: Tris (Shailene Woodley) and her father, Andrew Prior (Tony Goldwyn).

Left: Producers Doug Wick and Lucy Fisher study a scene with Kate Winslet (Jeanine Matthews).

"EVERY ONE OF US NEEDS TO CLAIM AN IDENTITY FOR OURSELVES AND FIGURE OUT WHO WE ARE, EVEN WHILE IT MEANS DIFFERENTIATING OURSELVES FROM OUR PARENTS."
—TONY GOLDWYN (ANDREW PRIOR)

In the film, Ashley Judd would play Goldwyn's wife, Natalie Prior. The two actors had worked together before, in *Someone Like You* as well as other films, so Goldwyn knew that they would be able to tap into the kind of affection that would make them seem convincing as a married couple. Judd was also ready to delve into the movie's other family relationships. "Right away we're introduced to these lovely siblings, a brother and sister who clearly are simpatico, and their futures lie in the balance," Judd says. "We can already see that Tris has great admiration, respect, and love for her parents. But she also has that dramatic conflict inside herself. . . ."

When Caleb and Tris both pick new factions at the Choosing Ceremony, Andrew and Natalie are left alone. But Natalie carries a secret: Once, she was Dauntless herself. Judd explains, "For whatever reason, my character hasn't found a compelling reason yet to tell her children that she was born into a different faction and chose to defect. Even when I do tell Tris, I don't unpack all of the information." At the end of the film, Tris is left with only the barest outline of her mother's history, and she can't ask Natalie any more questions.

"MY CHARACTER HASN'T FOUND A COMPELLING REASON YET TO TELL HER CHILDREN THAT SHE WAS BORN INTO A DIFFERENT FACTION AND CHOSE TO DEFECT."
—ASHLEY JUDD (NATALIE PRIOR)

Left: Natalie Prior (Ashley Judd).

Maggie Q, star of television's *Nikita*, signed on to play another important adult in Tris's world: Tori, who administers the aptitude test. Tori is the first to discover that Tris is Divergent, and later, the first to warn Tris that she's in danger. Tori has developed a hard exterior over her time in Dauntless, and at first she doesn't seem like an ally. As Maggie Q explains, "Tori's a vet. She's not one of the new kids. And she's this sort of mysterious character that becomes a guide for Tris."

An action star herself, Q was drawn to the action-packed script, but she also liked that the role would give her a chance to explore her softer side. "I like that idea of Tori being the unwilling mentor," she says. "The person who has knowledge that she doesn't want to share. Even though she's Dauntless, she has to come out of her space and sphere to be able to help someone. She doesn't really know Tris, but she connects to Tris's situation."

While Maggie Q would play a mentor, Ray Stevenson signed on to play Marcus, Four's abusive father. Stevenson had played a crime boss in *Dexter*, but he imagined Marcus as a more complicated character. "I wouldn't call Marcus the villain of the piece," Stevenson muses. "He sees in Four, maybe, too much reflection of himself."

As the Dauntless actors' training wrapped up, the other actors flew to Chicago to join them. Shooting on the film began in early April 2013, which meant that the sets and locations and costumes had to be ready, down to the last detail.

Above: Tori Wu (Maggie Q).

Left: Marcus Eaton (Ray Stevenson).

Above: Theo James as Detective Walter Clark in *Golden Boy* (2013).

Right: Tobias "Four" (Theo James).

While the rest of the cast was coming together, though, the search for Four continued. Producer Lucy Fisher remembers, "We kept saying, 'Who's Four? Who's Four?' We saw many leading men, and they were all interesting in their own way, but none was quite what we were looking for. It was difficult to find the perfect Four, to find somebody that could dominate Shailene, because she's so strong. We were getting near the end of our rope, sort of saying we don't know who the right person is. Then Theo James walked in and it was immediate; oh my . . . he's here. He did it. He did a chemistry reading with Shailene, and it knocked everybody out."

Author Veronica Roth adds, "The only screen test I saw was Theo's with Shailene, so I got to see their dynamic together, and they had incredibly good chemistry. After I saw it I was like, Please get him. Please! I was just

thrilled when he was cast and the deal closed because he was perfect. Amazing."

Adult audiences would know the young English actor from his brief, but critically important, role as Mr. Pamuk in the television series *Downton Abbey*. Younger audiences might recognize him from the film *Underworld: Awakening*, or his work in television series like *Bedlam* and *Golden Boy*. A starring role in *Divergent*, though, would give him much wider exposure and a new degree of fame. Those possibilities appealed to James, but what really drew him to the movie was the character himself.

James says, "I love that Four is a person who thinks before he speaks, who holds back—he's a watchful person. He's listening and watching, but he doesn't always feel like he needs to speak or to throw his weight around. Four has an old-school quality, a stillness and strength."

When he first read with Woodley, he remembers, Neil Burger warned him that Woodley would push back, challenge him. As predicted, she was forceful in her reading, but James was able to stand up to her. That was one important part of his character, James decided—his power and bravery. The other was his ability to be honest. James says, "When they're on the Ferris wheel, climbing up, Tris asks 'Are you scared?' And Four is supposed to be this masculine tough guy, but instead of denying it, he's straight about it. He says, 'Yes, I'm scared,' knowing that everyone is afraid of something. The fact that he's so comfortable with himself, that he can admit his own weaknesses, somehow makes him seem even stronger." James was able to connect with both sides of the character, the fierce and the vulnerable.

"Casting the right actors for the lead roles of *Divergent* was one of the most crucial elements that we needed to make sure was right," remembers Patrick Wachsberger, co-chairman of Lionsgate Motion Picture Group. "We took our time and were very thoughtful to find the right pair that could portray Tris and Four and the chemistry presented by Veronica Roth in her book. When Shailene Woodley and Theo James auditioned, their connection to the characters and each other was instant. Individually they are both very talented, but together they have a dynamic that matched exactly what was needed to tell our story. Their performances are brilliant in this film and we know fans of the book, as well as moviegoers who will be introduced to this story for the first time, will quickly fall in love with the pair."

"FOUR HAS AN OLD-SCHOOL QUALITY, A STILLNESS AND STRENGTH."
—THEO JAMES (FOUR)

TRAINING

LEARNING TO FIGHT

With their ensemble of actors complete, Burger and the producers called them together in Chicago to begin a sort of initiation of their own. They would need to get to know their parts and come together as a group, but most importantly they would need to get into the kind of physical shape that would mark them as Dauntless. As Miles Teller puts it, "This was not some actor training; this was legitimate body training."

Stunt coordinator Garrett Warren was their coach and choreographer. He recalls, "I had worked with Neil on *Limitless*, and he called asking me to come up with another inventive and ingenious fight style. Later, we sat down to talk about how we could do this. Stance was one way. Usually people have a regular fighting stance with their hands up—we wanted to do something that differentiated it. So we have the two hands folded in the front. We also worked on using a hammer fist rather than a regular punch. The hammer fist

is supposed to be something that generates a little more velocity, a little more force—and also saves the bony prominences on your hand."

In addition to mastering this uniquely Dauntless style of fighting, the actors learned the individual steps of their many fight sequences. Shailene Woodley and Miles Teller, as Tris and Peter, had to be careful as they worked through their choreography. Woodley says, "Neither of us had done stunt fights before. They're all very mechanical and timed . . . if I swing too hard, then I could actually hurt Miles, and if he swings too hard, he could actually hurt me. So we had to be tough onscreen but also compassionate toward each other as actors, recognizing that we could cause each other harm if we weren't gentle."

Left: Director Neil Burger and Shailene Woodley (Tris) discuss the Dauntless fighting stance.

Above: Tris (Shailene Woodley) fights Peter (Miles Teller) as Four (Theo James) looks on.

Not all the young actors were required to do the training. Ansel Elgort arrived in Chicago later than the others because his character is not Dauntless. And Jai Courtney, who plays Eric, says, "There's actually not that much action in this movie for me personally. I kind of managed to skip boot camp on this production, which I wasn't too upset about."

For the others, though, the training was an opportunity to build strength as well as character. Theo James, for instance, stayed apart from the others during training, because Four is supposed to be in a superior position. Although they're all about the same age, he is in a position of authority. Christian Madsen remembers a particular day, when "we had to do this training stuff with extras they'd brought in to be Dauntless members, and we're all together, and Theo came out as Four. He came out yelling at everybody, made Shai drop down and do twenty push-ups, and he was just . . . Four. It helps you out later, when you're shooting the scene, and you revert back to remembering how he treated everyone."

With Garrett Warren's guidance, the actors grew stronger and felt more fully developed as members of the Dauntless faction. As Ben Lloyd-Hughes puts it, "It's always good to have a coach there, telling you what to do and pushing you further. Those guys can help you achieve more physically than you ever could on your own in a gym." Even for characters with little dialogue in the *Divergent* script, it was important that they get to a place where they could seem physically threatening.

"THIS WAS NOT SOME ACTOR TRAINING;
THIS WAS LEGITIMATE BODY TRAINING."
—MILES TELLER (PETER)

Left: Four (Theo James) gives a demonstration with a Dauntless initiate.

Above: Shailene Woodley (Tris) and Miles Teller (Peter) film a scene with guidance from stunt coordinator Garrett Warren.

BUILDING THE WORLD
OF *DIVERGENT*

SCOUTING LOCATIONS

The Navy Pier Grand Ballroom is the setting for the final test of the fear landscapes.

Location manager James McAllister had been working around the clock. "I would say we probably scouted a hundred or more locations, and used about half," he says. "Neil was trying to find a lot of places that you would still see a hundred and fifty years from now, but used in a different way. The plaza we used for the high school, at the Michigan Avenue Bridge, is in a location that could still be a center of the city, well into the future. If a location felt too much like it had been seen in other films, though, Neil wanted to stay away from it, or look at it from a new perspective."

As McAllister scouted for locations, he kept in mind what the filmmakers would need to do to transform them for shooting. He explains, "We discussed the city streets and how best to give them the look of a hundred and fifty years from now. What kinds of present-day elements would we have to deal with? Traffic signals, lines in the streets, trash cans, bike racks, city street signs . . . all those things would have to go." Since the future in *Divergent* would be mostly free of cars, the production team would need to make the streets look unused or in disrepair, so ordinary items like signs and crosswalks would be extraneous. Some would be removed before

Top: The Seventeenth Church of Christ, Scientist, is the setting for the Choosing Ceremony.

Bottom: Director Neil Burger visualizes a shot.

the shoot, and some would be removed much later, in postproduction by a team led by visual effects supervisor Jim Berney.

"The visual effects in *Divergent* are subtle. We're taking the real city of Chicago a little bit into the future, but not so far out that your brain can't really wrap around it, but just enough to where it makes it a little eerie," says visual effects supervisor Jim Berney.

Chicago offered a broad range of places to choose from. In a city that grew from an industrial powerhouse to a world capital, there were a variety of opportunities. McAllister remembers, "Because of the position of Chicago in the Industrial Revolution, there was a lot of that type of structure here. Heavy steelwork and brick and big old factories. And because of the forward motion of the city, there's new and glossy, so you can get that, too."

One by one, he and Burger identified locations where they could shoot scenes. The Seventeenth Church of Christ, Scientist, in downtown Chicago, would make a majestic Choosing room. The Mansueto Library, at the University of Chicago, would be perfect for the Erudite library. The Ferris wheel at Navy Pier, a key part of Roth's story, would be available for the team to use—and so would the Grand Ballroom at the end of the Pier, which would accommodate an intimidating fear landscape.

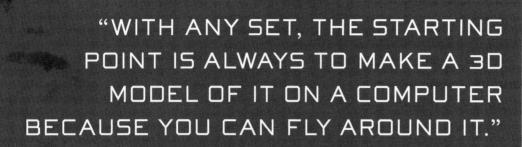

> "WITH ANY SET, THE STARTING POINT IS ALWAYS TO MAKE A 3D MODEL OF IT ON A COMPUTER BECAUSE YOU CAN FLY AROUND IT."
> —PRODUCTION DESIGNER ANDY NICHOLSON

At the same time, McAllister was starting to get a sense of what the film crew could shoot within the Chicago system of elevated trains—the Chicago "El." He recalls, "We had lengthy meetings with the transit authority, to talk about what we could and couldn't do on their property. We were able to start some of the climbing up the El structures, with very strict parameters on how high we could get and how many columns and distances from power lines."

As the scouting process wore on, and Neil Burger's team was in place, it became clear that the city would not offer perfect locations for every scene. Those that couldn't be shot at an existing site would be shot at sets they would build from the ground up. Many of them could be created at Cinespace, an enormous film production complex on the city's west side that offered cavernous spaces, paint and carpentry shops, and ample room for storage.

Whether they were looking at locations or planning sets, the filmmakers did painstaking planning before they brought in any cameras. Early in the process, production designer Andy Nicholson worked with a concept artist to create images of everything from the Dauntless headquarters to the skyline of Roth's future Chicago. "We needed to know what we were talking about—when we were standing on the street location, eventually, with cameras and costumes."

In addition, Nicholson did elaborate digital modeling of every set that was to be built. He explains, "With any set, the starting point is always to make a 3D model of it on a computer

because you can fly around it. You can put film lenses on it. You can do time-of-day studies for it. And all of those things become incredibly important when you're spending a large amount of someone else's money, say, building a big village outside. It's important that it works practically for shooting."

Left: Tris (Shailene Woodley) climbs the El structures leading to the trains.

Above: Chicago of the future.

Below: A 3D model of one of the El trains.

A HOME FOR EACH FACTION

One of the filmmakers' biggest challenges was distinguishing the identities of the different factions and conveying critical information about them from visual clues. Each faction's living and working quarters, costumes, and makeup needed to reflect and communicate their core values. In the film, audiences see how Abnegation and Dauntless live, with just a glimpse of Erudite and the factionless (and none of Amity or Candor at all). Burger and Nicholson imagined what the homes of each faction would look like. The Abnegation and Dauntless headquarters were the two largest sets the team built.

Production designer Andy Nicholson remembers, "One of the things we definitely tried to do with the creation of the factions was make them each appealing in their own way. Dauntless is obviously appealing. It's an exciting, dangerous, dynamic place to be. You kind of like the idea of Erudite as a place, even though they are the villains in the piece. And Tris finds Abnegation comfortable and calming until the moment she leaves—we hope that some people will watch the movie and think, Well, why did she leave Abnegation? It was kind of nice."

Amy Newbold, who plays Molly, remembers feeling a strong reaction to the locations chosen for the Dauntless compound. "These people are living in this completely utilitarian world where there's no frills," she explains, "yet everything was so detailed in these super cold warehouses."

A 3D model of the Dauntless Pit.

THE ABNEGATION VILLAGE

No location in Chicago lent itself naturally to an Abnegation neighborhood, so Burger and Nicholson agreed that they'd have to build one from scratch. The question was how to do it, and where. Ideally, they'd have space to create a group of Abnegation houses, where they could shoot exteriors for both the peaceful beginning and the violent end of the movie. The complex at Cinespace was an amazing resource for the film team, but it wasn't big enough to accommodate the final battle scene.

Executive producer John Kelly remembers, "So we came to Chicago, our first time out. Neil and I went up to the top of the Willis Tower—the Sears Tower. We stood on the 113th floor, the antennas are above us about three hundred feet high. And Neil looks down and he sees this little piece of ground maybe a mile away from the location we're at, and he goes, 'That's where we'll build Abnegation.' And I'm like, 'Well . . . if we can afford it. . . .' I didn't think it would work. It's a prime piece of land in downtown Chicago! But we got the location, and that's where we built our town. A humble Abnegation village in the shadow of one of the largest buildings in the world." Even though they were building a set, they were still taking full advantage of the city's best features.

The village was made up of a dozen compact gray houses with a simple, contemporary design. In the movie, it would look as if they were made from poured concrete, but they were really built from plaster, with decorative finishes. They were the very model of Abnegation's simplicity and modesty.

The Abnegation village with the Willis Tower in the background.

Creating the Abnegation village turned out to be an enormous task, involving three solid months of construction at the site. When it was finished, Burger's first instincts turned out to be dead-on. "The fact that it's a vacant property right on the edge of downtown, that was the big attraction to Neil," location manager McAllister explains. "We had looked at some other vacant land, six to eight blocks away, but it just gave a different perspective. That location, the city is right there, and it really fills the frame." Because the construction was out in the open, fans discovered it and came to watch the houses going up. Passersby who didn't know about *Divergent*, though, thought a new apartment complex was being built.

Above: Building the Abnegation village.

Right: An Abnegation home.

Below: Filming Shailene Woodley (Tris) atop the roof of the Priors' house.

INSIDE THE PRIORS' HOME

At Cinespace, another crew created the interior of Tris's house, which was modified to serve as the interior of other Abnegation houses as well. Set decorator Anne Kuljian explains, "What we've tried to do with the Abnegation set is reduce living to basic, common needs and necessities. One room functions as the dining area, the living area, and a working area for the family. The only other areas in the house are the kitchen and the bedrooms. So pretty much you're in this room 24-7 if you're home. We tried to set it up so that different activities could take place on one giant table. Sometimes eating, sometimes working, sometimes just talking. The confined set reflects the way the Abnegation think. Everything is very tight, and they live as a family unit."

The houses' color scheme also reflects the Abnegation aesthetic, Kuljian continues. "We tried to keep the elements at their most raw, and the color tones at their simplest. So we have the cool grays and we have the warm beige of the ash wood that we used quite a lot in this set. The set has a certain warmth, but it definitely feels minimalistic."

Even the floor of the house was emblematic of Abnegation's dedication to simplicity and recycled materials. Producer Lucy Fisher was on the set one day. "And there was this band of construction people in the Prior house, all excited. I came over and they were all beaming, so I said, 'What's going on?' They just said, 'Look at the floor.' And it was made up of a jigsaw puzzle of little pieces of wood, that supposedly would have been leftover pieces, and they perfectly fit. It was an exquisite floor, and it was so great because they were into the storytelling, too. They understood that the lock of Tris's hair would be cut and fall to that floor."

Below: Neil Burger directs the dinner scene at the Priors'.

Right: Shailene Woodley (Tris) and Ashley Judd (Natalie Prior) chat between takes. To their left are director of photography Alwin Küchler and director Neil Burger.

"THE SET HAS A CERTAIN WARMTH, BUT IT DEFINITELY FEELS MINIMALISTIC."
—SET DECORATOR ANNE KULJIAN

THE DAUNTLESS COMPOUND

Director Neil Burger prepares Theo James (Four) for a scene in the vast Dauntless Pit.

If the Abnegation set felt minimalist, the Dauntless set would need to feel raw yet vibrant. One challenge, though, was that it was also supposed to be underground. At first, production designer Andy Nicholson imagined a dark set, like a cave, but he knew it would be difficult to film in that kind of a space, since the characters would need to be lit while the background remained murky. Eventually Nicholson came to a novel idea. Rather than making the Dauntless headquarters a dark cave, he would make it a cave carved from marble or limestone.

Theo James, who plays Four, says, "When I read the book and the script for the first time, I thought of the cavern as a dark place. Wet and cold. And I wondered what drew the Dauntless there. It seemed so inhospitable, like they'd be cold all the time. Then Neil said that the white marble creates a sense of warmth, visually. And you really need that if you are going to buy into this world."

While the Pit, as the filmmakers called it, would look like it was underground, it was actually built on a massive soundstage at Cinespace. The construction required great time and effort, but the Pit had to be large enough to convey the freedom of the Dauntless, in contrast with the cramped Abnegation houses.

Dauntless group scenes would be filmed in the Pit and be augmented with scenes shot

at locations and sets styled to look like they were part of the same whole. Production designer Andy Nicholson explains, "You have a whole series of spaces that really have to work together for many different scenes and be identifiable and be interesting enough so it just doesn't look like you're shooting against walls without any background. So the corridors have very specific structures. It's very important for an audience to know where a character's gone to or come from."

Location manager James McAllister adds, "The whole Dauntless environment was tricky, because there were so many areas and elements to it. We needed to piece them all together so they meshed, while at the same time taking care not to make it all feel monotonous. Going to the dorm to the dining hall to the tunnel—each place had to look a little different." Different kinds of lighting, particularly LED lighting, helped to create these separate areas.

"THE FIGHTING ARENA WAS JUST ABOUT THE CHANCE TO USE A SPACE OF THAT SIZE AND TO TAKE ADVANTAGE OF THE PERSPECTIVE IT OFFERS. IT'S VERY INTERESTING TO BE IN A PLACE OF THAT SCALE WHEN IT HAS NOTHING IN IT AT ALL, BECAUSE PEOPLE REALLY DO DISAPPEAR AT THE OTHER SIDE OF THE BUILDING."
—PRODUCTION DESIGNER ANDY NICHOLSON

THE DAUNTLESS DINING HALL

While **postproduction work** would make it seem like the dining hall was within the Dauntless Pit, it was actually filmed at an entirely different location. "We went through several different choices before we found something that wasn't too big and wasn't too small to work," remembers Andy Nicholson. "We settled on the location we used because it had a fantastic ceiling light, and it was in a really great room that had two levels. It was enough to contain, I think, two hundred people without being enormous and without cramming them in too much. And there were areas you could come out of complete darkness into. It was like coming out of the cave and into this light area. That was what inspired us."

Location manager James McAllister adds, "It was a former athletic club from just after the turn of the century that had an indoor swimming pool with a track, but had long since been abandoned. When we scouted it, there was snow on the roof and leaking near the skylight, so we did some repairs. But of course the week that we shot the location we had probably the worst rainstorm in three years. It became an around-the-clock job, making sure the location was filmable, just keeping the water out."

Above and right: Director Neil Burger discusses a scene with the cast and crew.

THE DORMS

The Dauntless initiates live in the cold dormitory inside the Pit, all shiny surfaces and open space. There's no privacy here for the newcomers, not even in the bathrooms.

"The transfer dorm has the discomfort factor, which is helpful," recalls Amy Newbold. "There's such a clear vision for this Dauntless world that's shown up in every set. The dorms are super minimalistic and only have necessities."

"THE DAUNTLESS WORLD IS SO MINIMAL— SO RAW AND DIRTY AND GRITTY AND DARK."

—AMY NEWBOLD (MOLLY)

Left: Director of photography Alwin Küchler gets a close-up of Amy Newbold (Molly).

Above: Collaborating on a scene featuring Shailene Woodley (Tris): (L to R) B Camera/ Steadicam operator Dave Thompson; director of photography Alwin Küchler; camera operator Martin Schaer; and director Neil Burger.

While the initiates live in the dorm, those who have made it through initiation can live wherever they want. When Tris and Four are together in Four's apartment, it's one of the first times they have a chance to be alone. *Divergent* book fans were especially eager to know what Four's apartment would look like.

Director Neil Burger says, "Four's found a cool space aboveground that he's pulled together in a pretty great way." Andy Nicholson searched all over Chicago because, as he puts it, "I wanted to have somewhere that was semi-industrial but not completely. Eventually we discovered a fantastic mezzanine over a recording studio, which had a hundred-foot window down one side, which we treated the glass on. Then I just brought in some natural tin ceiling panels to use as walling and stuff like that. It had to be comfortable, romantic, and very uniquely his. It was as far from the dorm as we could get it."

It was Anne Kuljian's job to create the interior design for the apartment. She gave Four a random assortment of items he could have

> "FOUR'S FOUND A COOL SPACE ABOVEGROUND THAT HE'S PULLED TOGETHER IN A PRETTY GREAT WAY."
> —DIRECTOR NEIL BURGER

gathered from around the city. She explains, "The Dauntless can collect things from different parts of the past, and they can bring things together. Their look is much more eclectic, and their colors are much brighter."

Neil Burger says, "The Dauntless are really good scavengers as well as being good fighters. They've kind of cherry-picked all the coolest leftovers, whether they're furniture or lamps or other pieces of things, and brought them together into their world."

Left: Four (Theo James) in his apartment.

Above: Shailene Woodley (Tris) reads *Divergent* on the set of Four's loftlike apartment.

Right: Four's place—away from the dorms.

FEAR SIMULATIONS

Because the fear simulation sequences play such an important role in developing the characters of Tris and Four, Burger wanted to set them apart, visually, from the rest of the film, without doing anything that would be disruptive to the viewer. After experimenting with some options, he decided to shoot these scenes with an anamorphic lens that would distort the images slightly. Anytime Tris is under the influence of a serum—whether it's during the aptitude test or during her Dauntless initiation—the audience sees her world through the anamorphic lens. The viewer won't even realize what is off about the image at first, just that it is different from the images that came immediately before.

Although the Dauntless simulation room is small and simple, it feels dramatic. The image of a single chair in a cold environment is striking. Veronica Roth remembers the emotional impact of seeing it for the first time. She says, "It's weird, but the coolest day that I had was seeing the simulation room, which is funny because that's basically just a room with a chair in it, and a computer, and a syringe, and that's all. But the chair was this kind of gross orange color, and it had this ominous headpiece to keep people's heads in place. And then the syringe was this elaborate-looking torture device, and it was terrifying. I realized that every little detail of this is working together to make this situation seem as frightening to the audience as it is to the person sitting in the chair."

Above: Tris (Shailene Woodley) and Four (Theo James) during a fear simulation.

Right: Tris (Shailene Woodley) and Four (Theo James) enact one of Tris's fears: becoming intimate with Four.

In addition, Nicholson designed the simulation sequences so that each would take place in a smaller, more constrictive space, until he opened up into the final sequence, the fear landscape, which would be in a space many times bigger than the rest. "The only way you can visually sell that kind of idea onscreen," he explains, "is if you have a progression that's such a shock that it makes it all worthwhile."

The room where the characters wait before going into the fear sim room is small and linear, with a symmetrical light source. The fear sim room itself is only slightly bigger, with a couple of unusual details, like slanting doors, that the viewer won't really notice until Tris walks through them. She walks through a narrow corridor that opens up, then, into the larger fear landscape room, where she will face crows, a tank of water, the threat of being burned alive, the prospect of sex with Four, and the horrific task of killing her own family.

The fear landscape was filmed on location at the end of Chicago's Navy Pier, a landmark that stretches a mile out into Lake Michigan. Under a massive, eighty-foot dome sits one lone chair for Tris to settle into before the simulation begins. Audiences will feel her discomfort from the moment she sees the looming space and waits for the simulation to begin.

> "IT'S WEIRD, BUT THE COOLEST DAY THAT I HAD WAS SEEING THE SIMULATION ROOM."
> —AUTHOR VERONICA ROTH

THE FENCE

In Roth's novel, Andy Nicholson points out, you never know whether the fence around the city is keeping people in or keeping people out. You know it is there, but you don't know its size or function.

For the purposes of the film, Nicholson decided to make it a more striking feature. "I found a reference, a radar installation in Russia," he says, "which kind of sparked a lot of conversation. It became the basis for something that was so big that you didn't know what it was." There was only one problem. Could they find such a fence in real life?

Executive producer John Kelly tells the story like this: "In the book, there's a scene where the Dauntless initiates go to the fence and they climb up and they see outside of the city walls. I figured we'd be building something twenty-five feet high that looked like a big cement wall. But Neil said no, let's find a big wall. Okay. Problem is, there's no forty-foot wall in Chicago." Sure enough, though, location manager James McAllister managed

> ## "YOU NEVER KNOW WHETHER THE FENCE AROUND THE CITY IS KEEPING PEOPLE IN OR KEEPING PEOPLE OUT."
>
> —PRODUCTION DESIGNER ANDY NICHOLSON

to find a concrete wall—inside the city—that ran about a quarter of a mile long. Kelly continues, "So we get out there and it's part of an old steel factory, where they held a lot of materials that went into the manufacturing of steel. The wall is probably about forty feet high, probably fifteen feet wide, and is the perfect base for our walled city."

Left: The wall patrolled by Dauntless.

Below: Dauntless initiates reach the wall.

THE TRAINS

Below: Filming special effects train scenes using green screen.

Right: Filming a train scene with Theo James (Four) and Shailene Woodley (Tris).

Since there are few cars in the future Chicago of *Divergent*, trains are the main form of transportation. They take characters between the factions' different areas, circling the city in an endless loop.

When the film crew began discussion of how to handle the train sequences, they planned to create a train that could travel on the existing Chicago El tracks and structure. When they realized the number of practical problems that would cause, however, they decided to build their own train and sections of track instead. The train car was built on top of a bus chassis, which made it easy to move it from place to place.

In addition, they also built a small section of El structure, for when the Dauntless climb

up and wait for the train. Location manager James McAllister says, "We put our section of track in a canyon, so we could get some of that real city environment all around us."

The train sequences were shot in pieces and augmented with visual effects. (Special effects are flourishes, such as lights or smoke, that are created and then filmed by a camera. Visual effects are those that must be added after the shoot. Often there is a blank spot in the film—indicated by a green screen—that indicates something to be filled in later.) Visual effects producer Greg Baxter explains, "The first train sequence, when Tris leaves the Choosing Ceremony and runs with the Dauntless, gets onto the train, takes the train to the Dauntless compound, and jumps off . . . that sequence is probably one of our most expensive visual effects sequences. We had to film it in six different places. Our job is to tie it all together so the audience doesn't realize it was a location, and then a set piece, and then a stage, and then the back of our parking lot."

While they didn't always film on the real El, the actors really did jump on and off the train, and they worked hard to prepare for the train sequences.

Neil Burger planned these scenes with painstaking care. He recalls, "I sort of sketched out how I saw the scene, and these are very rough thumbnails to start with. That's somebody grabbing a handle, running away from us; those are feet running away from us. The whole scene is in very rough storyboards. And then I worked with a guy who drew them in a quicker way, and we turned those into the pre-visualization, which basically looks like a video game, or something like that. It allows us to know where we need green screen, which parts will need visual effects, and which parts we can do for real, what we need to build and what we don't need to build. That way, we can

be really efficient when shooting. We know we're looking from the front of the train to the back, we're going to need some sort of green screen beyond the train because we're going to put the city in, and sometimes we're looking into the train so we don't need that at all. It's a matter of knowing what we're going to shoot, how we're going to tell the story, and what tools we're going to do it with."

> "THAT SEQUENCE IS PROBABLY ONE OF OUR MOST EXPENSIVE VISUAL EFFECTS SEQUENCES. WE HAD TO FILM IT IN SIX DIFFERENT PLACES."
> —VISUAL EFFECTS PRODUCER GREG BAXTER

DAUNTLESS
DIVERGENT 2013

CANDOR
BACKGROUND
DIVERGENT 2013

19

DAUNTLESS ②
FINALE
DIVERGENT 2012

A LOOK FOR EACH FACTION:
COSTUMES AND MAKEUP

The **futuristic tone** of the movie and the core values of the different factions would also be expressed through costume and makeup design. In other movies, great attention is given to creating a unique look for each character; in *Divergent*, however, the focus was on developing a look that worked for whole groups of characters—the factions—while still allowing for a range of differences within each group.

Costume designer Carlo Poggioli was charged with articulating the factions' styles in a very short time frame. He signed on to work on the film in January 2013, and shooting would begin in Chicago three months later. Within that time, he needed both to create the looks for the factions and arrange to manufacture large numbers of costumes.

"The challenge to understanding a futuristic world is understanding just how futuristic you want it to be," Poggioli explains. "Neil was telling me from the beginning that this future is not so far away from today. I needed to keep the futuristic designs rooted in now, so the audiences could connect with the costumes." Poggioli had a lot of experience working on

Left: Costume designer Carlo Poggioli.

Above: An Amity outfit prototype.

historic films, from *The English Patient* and *Cold Mountain* to *Abraham Lincoln: Vampire Hunter*. His most recent project had been Terry Gilliam's film *The Zero Theorem*, but he was still quite new to science fiction and had never had the chance to invent an entirely new world through costume design. "It was the first movie where I made everything from the clothes to the accessories, even some of the shoes," he says.

Poggioli began with a series of sketches informed by the brief descriptions in Roth's book. While she had described the colors for each faction, she had not described the shapes of their clothes, or considered the way they would work when real people were wearing them. It was up to Poggioli to make her ideas three-dimensional. Once he had sketched out some ideas, he began a series of long calls with Burger, Wick, and Fisher, from his base in Rome.

"THE CHALLENGE TO UNDERSTANDING A FUTURISTIC WORLD IS UNDERSTANDING JUST HOW FUTURISTIC YOU WANT IT TO BE."
—COSTUME DESIGNER CARLO POGGIOLI

Costume designer Carlo Poggioli's sketches of Amity's clothing.

— CHOOSING CEREMONY — AMITY —
"DIVERGENT" 2012

DRESSING DAUNTLESS

It was urgent that they develop the Dauntless look first, because most of the characters were Dauntless, and many of the Dauntless sequences would be shooting first. "We didn't want to represent them in uniforms, like soldiers," Poggioli remembers. "Neil directed me away from the idea that this was a militaristic society." Instead, Burger was looking for something exuberant, youthful, cool, intense, and a bit mysterious.

As in the book, basic black was the way to go. The color could say punk rock or high fashion, or anything in between—many different kinds of brave people wear black. And black would also be functional for characters who were in constant motion. The costumes were made of a special fabric Poggioli had developed specifically for the Dauntless. It was flexible, like athletic clothes, but not made of Lycra, and it appears to be recycled, like so much in the *Divergent* world. All of the Dauntless fabric had to be tested to make sure it would work in the action scenes, and some actors received extra gussets—flexible patches of fabric—in their clothes to allow extra movement.

—TRIS—②
"DIVERGENT" 2013
Gio Poli

Above: A sketch of Tris's uniform and fabric samples.

Right: A prototype of a Dauntless uniform designed for Tris.

Opposite: A full-color sketch of female Dauntless uniforms.

DAUNTLESS ③

To differentiate the groups within the faction, Poggioli came up with a set of colors to accent the black. Transfers, for instance, have orange accents, while Dauntless-born have red. Dauntless trainers have purple accents. These accents serve as reference colors for the audience, allowing them to keep track of each character's place in the hierarchy.

Poggioli recalls what happened next. "I made the prototypes in Rome where I live, and I brought the prototypes to workshops I knew in Hungary and Romania—I mean, we had to make thousands of costumes. We started on the thirteenth of February and had our first shipment on the thirteenth of March. In one month, they did all the Dauntless and the Abnegation—it was just unbelievable."

Left: A male Dauntless uniform prototype.

Right: Dauntless faction uniforms shown in many subtle shades.

ABNEGATION'S SIMPLICITY

The Abnegation clothing was completely different, made from natural fabrics and with a simple shape. "Not too much color," Poggioli says. "Mostly grays, because they're not interested in vanity. It's a rough cut, too . . . the shape of the Abnegation is a little like a sack." For many characters, he mixed light fabrics, such as linen, with heavy fabrics, such as wool.

> ## "YOU KNOW, THEY'RE NOT JUST PIECES THAT THE CHARACTERS WEAR, THEY'RE ALMOST CHARACTERS WITHIN THEMSELVES. THEY HELP TO TELL THE STORY VISUALLY."
> —SHAILENE WOODLEY (TRIS)

Because the Abnegation value modesty, their costumes show very little skin. Tris is covered up like the others at the beginning of the movie (though she regards the Dauntless with curiosity at school). "As she transforms into Dauntless," Poggioli says, "we begin to discover her body. We begin to discover her skin." Her later costumes are more body-conscious and fashion-forward. In this way, the costumes help to tell the story without words. As Shailene Woodley puts it, "You know, they're not just pieces that the characters wear, they're almost characters within themselves. They help to tell the story visually."

Above: A sketch of Abnegation costumes.

Right: Faction members dressed in Abnegation gray.

ABNEGATION BACKGROUND DIVERGENT 2013

Above: Costume designer Carlo Poggioli adjusting an Abnegation costume on set.

Below: A sketch of Abnegation costumes.

CHOOSING CEREMONY — ABNEGATION —
"DIVERGENT" 2012

(13)

BEATRICE ①

ABNEGATION
"DIVERGENT" 2013

CALEB

ABNEGATION
"DIVERGENT"

Original sketches aren't too far from how Tris (Shailene Woodley) and Caleb (Ansel Elgort) dress in *Divergent*.

THE SHARP LOOK OF THE ERUDITE

The basic idea for the Erudite clothing came from Neil Burger himself: a scientist's lab coat, with a functional cut and plenty of pockets. "This was a difficult concept for me at first," Poggioli remembers, "because I thought they would look too much like uniforms. But he was right, because we were able to do many variations." The Erudite clothing had a cold color palette of blues—which supposedly sharpen the mind—and crisp tailoring. The coats were modified for different groups inside the faction as well.

One kind of lab-inspired coat would work for wearing outside, for instance, and another would be worn by the faction's technical team. Poggioli points out, "Kate Winslet's coat is a little different from the others, because she's allowed to wear the green accent underneath the blue. She looks like she's wearing the same thing as the others, but she's not—the little details are completely different, like the inside of the collar of her coat." In addition, the length of Winslet's coat concealed the fact that she was five months pregnant.

DIVERGENT 2013

JANINE ④

LAB COAT IN RUBBER
BLU - SEMI TRNSP.
HEADQUARTER

DIVERGENT 2013

NEW EURIDITE
LAB COAT ⑬
FOR LAB WORKERS

(IN BLUE
RUBBER
SEMI TRANSPARENT)

This page: Erudite costume sketches with fabric samples.

OPPOSITE PAGE:
Top: Erudite faction members in costume.

Bottom left: A male Erudite uniform prototype.

Bottom right: Caleb Prior (Ansel Elgort) clothed in his Erudite uniform and Tris Prior (Shailene Woodley) dressed in Dauntless.

THE CONTRAST OF CANDOR

While we don't see much of Candor or Amity in this film, great care went into their respective looks. "Candor was the most difficult faction to design," says Poggioli. "The idea was to have them in black and white, because that's what comes from the book. But I started off in a completely wrong direction. I was thinking that the Candor were the open faction . . . I was thinking about transparency, different colors of glass, maybe sea glass . . . but it didn't work, even with a special shape for Candor. Neil decided, in the end, it was better to stick with black and white." The focus in Candor is not on either color but on the contrast between the two. If a character wears a white jacket, they have black pants. If they have a white vest, they have a black jacket. And of course, in Candor we see no shades of gray.

Top left: Sketches of Candor uniforms.

Bottom left: Christina (Zoë Kravitz) in the Candor uniform based on the prototype to the right.

THE FRIENDLY LOOK OF AMITY

Amity characters wear natural fabrics—presumably from fibers they grow themselves, like cotton—that are colored with vegetable dyes. And the factionless wear costumes that hint at the characters' past factions, their colors faded to only a shadow of what they used to be. These groups' looks will get more screen time and be developed further in later films.

Left: Sketches of Amity children's costumes.

Above: An Amity costume prototype.

Top: Sketches of Amity costumes.

Below: The Amity faction in costume on set.

MANUFACTURING THE COSTUMES: A MASSIVE UNDERTAKING

While the costumes were manufactured en masse in Europe, Poggioli also found a local crew in Chicago to create costumes for the lead characters and handle fittings for the large group scenes. The largest scene in the movie is the Choosing Ceremony, which required seven hundred extras from all the factions. Each costume was made by hand in the overseas workshops and finished in Chicago, after being fitted to an individual actor or extra. Poggioli's team then added details to distinguish, for instance, the adults from the children. It was a massive undertaking.

Poggioli worked closely with production designer Andy Nicholson because, as he says, "When you think about how to create a costume, you have to think about where that costume will go. The character you're creating is moving where? If the costume goes into a space that has nothing to do with the colors or the kind of fabric you've used, then you've made it wrong."

Above: Members of each faction are easily distinguished by their clothing.

Top left: Author Veronica Roth visits the costume department on set with costume shop supervisor Giovanni Lipari.

Bottom Left: Production designer Andy Nicholson shares his work with director Neil Burger.

Above: A touch-up by makeup department head Brad Wilder.

Right: The makeup team created the Dauntless tattoos.

TATTOOS, PIERCINGS, AND HARDWARE

Carlo Poggioli also collaborated with Brad Wilder and Denise Paulson of the makeup department. The Abnegation wore no makeup—or the appearance of no makeup—while the Erudite were carefully groomed and polished. They wore blue eye makeup, blue or black eyeliner, and nail polish in various shades of blue. All the Erudite men were clean shaven.

The idea for the Amity makeup was inspired by the hippie-era flower children circa 1968: fuller hair for the women, long hair and beards for the men. Their makeup had a pretty, soft palette of pinks and peaches, with eyes in rust and gold. The Candor palette was more neutral, with soft gray and brown eye shadow, lips in rich colors, and natural nails.

And naturally, the Dauntless look was the boldest and most edgy, with green or black eye shadow and extensive piercings. Makeup department head Brad Wilder was inspired by wandering around a hardware store and realizing that, in a future society, jewelry might be defined very differently. In addition to ordinary piercings, some characters, such as Eric, have studs (created by hardware bolts) embedded in their skin. (Or really, stuck to the skin with double-sided tape.) To the studs, Wilder attached different, interchangeable kinds of nuts. The hardware store also inspired the earrings worn by Maggie Q as Tori—they are made of washers, nuts, and bolts, held together with wire—and Eric's earrings, created from rubber compression nuts.

Tattoos were the final piece of the Dauntless look. Director Neil Burger says, "It seems like everyone has a tattoo now, so I wanted to come up with a way that the Dauntless tattoos were a little bit different. So I came up with this idea that they're blood tattoos, that somehow they're the pigments of your skin that form the design. To get the tattoo, they put a toxin into your skin that basically releases the pigmentation, whether it's the purple of a bruise or the red of your blood, and they've figured out how to do it in a very focused way to create a particular design."

Below left: Tris's famous tattoo: three birds (Shailene Woodley).

Below right: Eric (Jai Courtney), tattooed and pierced.

Designs for these blood tattoos—from the faction markers to the ravens on Tris's neck—were created by the film's art department, who then made them into transferable tattoos that could be refreshed for shooting every day.

Like the rest of the costumes and makeup, the tattoos create character without words. When Tris is tattooed with three birds to remind her of the three family members she's left behind, the audience is constantly aware of that choice, although Tris never mentions it again. And when viewers see the tip of a tattoo on Four's neck, it creates a mystery and hints at a question: What is underneath? With each design detail, the filmmakers add dimension and depth to their story.

Working on Theo James's (Four) tattoos are (L to R) head of makeup Brad Wilder, additional makeup artist Zsofia Otvos, and key makeup artist Denise Paulson.

SHOOTING THE FILM

LONG DAYS

Above: Author Veronica Roth looks at the screen with producer Lucy Fisher.

Right: Stunt coordinator Garrett Warren attaches a safety line to a harness underneath Shailene Woodley's (Tris) costume.

Production on the film began in early April. For over three months, the cast and crew crisscrossed the city of Chicago, shooting the *Divergent* film scene by scene. As with any movie, the scenes weren't shot chronologically, so it would be difficult for an outside observer or a person on the street to get a sense of the growing whole. At the end of each day, though, director Neil Burger and his team watched the dailies—raw footage of the day's work—and they could see that the film was becoming all they had hoped for, and more.

For Shailene Woodley, the days were exhilarating but long. Most cast members came in and out of scenes, but she was in every one of them. It was a heavy workload for the actress, but nobody saw her falter. Executive producer John Kelly says, "If we're starting at the beginning of the week, she's in at five thirty in the morning. She comes to set. She does rehearsal with the rest of the cast and the director and crew and then she goes, she gets her makeup on. She gets her wardrobe on. She comes back out. We start the scene and we go through and we start. We're going to go until six o'clock, seven o'clock at night. She's going to get out of makeup about seven thirty. She's going to get home at eight o'clock. And then sometimes she's got to be back at six a.m. to do it all again. Usually if you're an actor you do one scene, maybe go back to your trailer and you can take a nap, relax, sort of just rejuvenate. But not Shailene. And there's days where, when we were doing the running in this train, she ran back and forth probably forty times. Probably ran a hundred yards forty times during the day, had to do her scenes, had to be ready, had to look fresh every take, and she was absolutely fantastic about how she dealt with it and how she treated everybody."

Woodley wasn't complaining, because the role was a dream come true. Not only was her character the focal point of a major film, but she was working with an extraordinary group of actors—some world-famous—and learning from them every day. In addition, she and Neil Burger had a productive working relationship, where they could exchange ideas honestly. "Neil sees this movie in a very visual way," says Woodley, "where I'm used to doing movies where it's more character-driven, from a heart-based point of view. So it's really great to have both those parts together. He'll say, 'I need you to do a game face—you're serious right now,' and I'm like, 'No, Neil, she's a vulnerable little girl, she's not serious right now.' And we're able to hear each other and sort of meet halfway."

"IF WE'RE STARTING AT THE BEGINNING OF THE WEEK, SHE'S IN AT FIVE THIRTY IN THE MORNING."
—PRODUCER JOHN KELLY

Visits from author Veronica Roth kept the actors focused and alive, as they were performing the scenes she had written. And Roth, for her part, couldn't get enough of watching. She describes the experience like this: "Mostly I was in awe. Filming movies is very repetitive—for a single two-minute scene, they get a series of takes from one angle, then rearrange everything and get a series of takes from another angle, so it can take hours. I think everyone was expecting me to get tired of that repetition, but I never did. Whenever I went to the set, I stayed until the bitter end, if I could—it's completely fascinating and surreal and wonderful to watch the world in your brain become physical and

active in that way. I did get emotional on certain days, when I saw certain things. The day of one of the significant character deaths (I don't want to spoil!) was also deeply upsetting, simply because Shailene Woodley is amazing and really dug deep. That scene was raw and intense; it completely gutted me. I rode home on the train that day, instead of getting a ride, just so I could collect myself and mull it over."

While the actors had worked hard in training, the filming of the fight sequences was a completely different experience. Producer Doug Wick remembers, "It was startling when we first saw one of the fight scenes cut together. Neil shot it very much from Shai's

> **"IT WAS STARTLING WHEN WE FIRST SAW ONE OF THE FIGHT SCENES CUT TOGETHER."**
> —Producer Doug Wick

point of view, and the idea of going into the ring, where there's a guy there who's bigger and wants to hurt you . . . and seeing her go up against it in a real way and recover from that experience . . . that was extreme."

The fighting was hard on all the actors, not just Woodley. Zoë Kravitz describes it like this: "You start and stop in training . . . we'd run it a few times and then we'd stop. But when you're shooting, you only have a certain amount of time to get the fight scene done, and I got really tired! Which is great, you know, because you kind of want some desperation to come through in the scene."

Veronica Roth was on set for one of the Dauntless training days, when Tris and the others are learning to shoot guns. She remembers, "We were on this really dirty, dusty rooftop and the wind was blowing the dirt around, so everyone's faces were coated in grime, dirt caked into every pore. That night I put my hand through my hair and it stood straight up without any assistance. I found particles of dirt in my ear for days afterward."

Left: Author Veronica Roth chats with executive producer Rachel Shane during a visit to the set.

Below: Shailene Woodley (Tris) and Miles Teller (Peter) film a fight scene.

Shailene Woodley (Tris)
and Theo James (Four)
film a fight scene.

DO I DO MY OWN STUNTS?

As the days went on and the cast members built up a new level of comfort and trust with one another, many of them felt that their performances were growing stronger. "As Shailene and I became closer as friends, the scenes were kind of developing in that way anyway," says Theo James. "When we didn't know each other . . . we could use that. And then when we became more at ease in each other's company and in each other's body language, we could use that, too."

Many of the young actors were eager to try their own stunts, and stunt coordinator Garrett Warren did all he could to accommodate their interest while still keeping them safe. Theo James says, "I'm glad that, whenever we could, we were allowed to do our own stunts because (a) they're the fun parts, and (b) you can feed off of that kind of energy and create something good out of it." Warren adds, "Safety is always a boundary on a movie set. When we first discuss any of these stunts, safety is always the first thing that comes up. But we also have to make it seem—to the audience—that this is a little bigger and a little badder than anything they have seen. In the future, you know, you have to go a little bit bigger than you would now."

Shailene Woodley—like Tris herself—was facing some fears as she made the movie. She says, "I don't have a fear of heights . . . I have a fear of falling. But it's one of those things that I get so pumped by that I have to continue to do it. I get such an adrenaline rush from completing something that I didn't think I could complete." Woodley used her fear—and her search for the adrenaline high—to bring real feeling to the scene where Tris takes the first jump into the Dauntless Pit. In spite of her fears, Woodley did the first part of the jump herself.

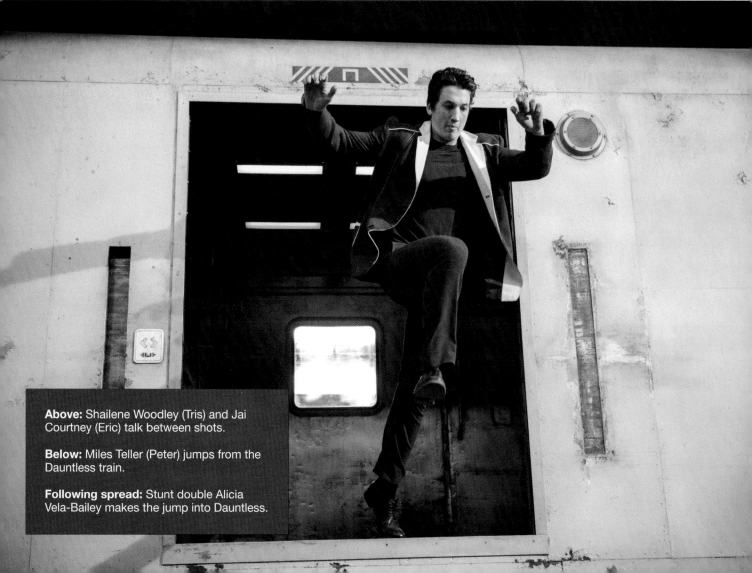

Above: Shailene Woodley (Tris) and Jai Courtney (Eric) talk between shots.

Below: Miles Teller (Peter) jumps from the Dauntless train.

Following spread: Stunt double Alicia Vela-Bailey makes the jump into Dauntless.

Garrett Warren explains, "As much as visual effects can do a great job of re-creating a scene, it's not the same thing as the real thing. You will never see a person fall with the same kind of weight in a two-dimensional character as you would with a three-dimensional person." Woodley stood at the top of a real building in Chicago, seventy feet up, in high winds. She was wearing safety cables and had a team of people there to protect her, but she was the one leaping from the ledge . . . over and over again. Neil Burger says, "So she's jumped on a train, she's jumped off a train, and now Tris has to jump down through this seven-story courtyard through a hole in which she has no idea what's at the bottom. We've already shot her landing, at a different building, but this is from the top. Shailene is game for anything, so she wants to do the jump herself."

The full jump was actually performed by Woodley's fearless stunt double, Alicia Vela-Bailey, whose personal record had been a thirty-foot jump before she signed on for *Divergent*. Slowly, Garrett Warren worked her up to becoming comfortable with the seventy-foot jump that was required. Warren says, "Even though that air bag might be nine feet tall and eighteen feet wide, it looks like a cell phone when you're jumping off a seventy-foot building, and to miss that air bag is the end of the world. We also wanted to play with how she could act when she was doing it, because nobody just wants to see a stunt person jump off a building. You want to see Tris jump off a building!" As Vela-Bailey hurtled through the air, Warren was in front of her with a camera to catch the action.

Below: Shailene Woodley (Tris) takes a photo as her stunt double completes the jump into Dauntless. The camera man in the sky is stunt coordinator Garrett Warren.

Right: Shailene Woodley (Tris) and her stunt double, Alicia Vela-Bailey, mug for the camera.

DAUNTING FOR DAUNTLESS

Every day on the set was physically demanding for the Dauntless. For instance, says Garrett Warren, "On the train sequence, we had to have them jump from the train across a wall. We first set the train at a six-foot distance and wanted to drive it at eight miles an hour. Safe for everyone to do, and we had everyone train for it. But on the day that we got there, Neil looked at it and said, yeah, that's good, but it would be nice if we could go bigger than that and make it a little bit more scary. We ended up moving the wall out to eight feet, and we drove at twelve miles per hour."

Of Woodley, Warren says, "I'm not surprised that she's able to do as much as she has, but I am surprised with how fast she recovers because, you know, to run and catch a train at twelve miles an hour is exhausting, and to do that all day long is really exhausting. But she comes back in and she's ready to go, so I give her a lot of credit."

The cold, wet weather in Chicago's not-quite-spring was a factor the production team had to contend with. The Dauntless dining hall scene, for instance, was created in spite of the constant threat of flooding. Once they were ready to go, though, cast and crew continued working—on this scene and others—as long as it was safe.

A physically demanding train scene.

Huddling—the Dauntless actors and director Neil Burger during a cold day of shooting.

Neil Burger recalls an instance when the weather could have really messed up a shoot: "So it's the second-to-last scene in the movie, where Tris and her brother and some others are really running to get out of Dauntless. Working with trains, even when you've made your own, is always a bit dangerous—they're huge, heavy machines—and these guys are running to get on. There's not a great way to hang on, and now it's raining, which makes it more dangerous. We've got huge cranes in the air, holding up an assortment of lights and silks and green screens . . . if the wind comes up, they'll all blow over, and if the lightning comes up, they'll all be lightning rods, so it's all a little hairy . . . luckily, none of that stuff happened. We sort of dodged a bullet and got the scene done."

Shooting the scenes beside the fence also was tricky. "We get out there next to the wall, and we're in the middle of a field—and right next to Lake Michigan," John Kelly says. "And when I say lake, you know, it's like a small sea, or an ocean. It has high waves, tankers, everything. So we're out there and we're getting winds, like, twenty miles an hour. Hair is blowing. Carts are rolling, things are just going everywhere. And that's before we start getting wind gusts, fifteen-foot whitecaps on the lake. It was crazy. We shot through it, though. All done safely."

"I'M NOT SURPRISED THAT SHE'S ABLE TO DO AS MUCH AS SHE HAS, BUT I AM SURPRISED WITH HOW FAST SHE RECOVERS."
—STUNT COORDINATOR GARRETT WARREN

THE FERRIS WHEEL, CAPTURE THE FLA
AND THE ZIP LINE

Shailene Woodley and Theo James shot their pivotal scene on the Ferris wheel from midnight to five in the morning. Burger's team had worked hard to reserve time for filming at Chicago's Navy Pier, a popular tourist destination. Within one night, they needed to age the area to make it look as if it had been abandoned for fifty or sixty years—adding dirt, moss, gravel, and rust—do the filming, and then restore everything to normal before the tourists arrived the next day. It was a huge undertaking, made even more intense by the cold that night. "It was a real element of testing," remembers Theo James. His hands were almost sticking to the bars, and he and Woodley stayed

at the top of the Ferris wheel for almost two hours, shooting the scene about forty times.

In spite of the cold, though, Shailene Woodley remembers that night fondly. "The Ferris wheel looks way more complicated and intense than it really was," she says. "We were on a ladder that was not completely vertical—more like a forty-five-degree angle. And we were attached to safety lines and it was fun. It was beautiful, too. . . . That night there was a full moon, and it was the first lunar eclipse of the year. So Theo and I got to experience that magical moment, climbing up—which I'm not sure he cared about, but I thought it was pretty great."

Above and at left: The Ferris wheel scene with Theo James (Four) and Shailene Woodley (Tris).

While this important scene could be created with real actors at a real place, some of the other critical scenes were heavier on effects and required careful behind-the-scenes planning as well as strong performances by the actors against green screens. Visual effects producer Greg Baxter explains, "In Four's fear landscape, when he's on the high wire, we had him on a wire between existing skyscrapers, but obviously we're not going to put him way up there. We have our actors on a green screen stage on a wire with a pad below them in case they fall off, and that entire environment is computer generated. But it has to look exactly like you took a photograph of those buildings on, you know, noon on a Saturday."

When Tris zip lines off Chicago's Hancock building, also, the scene is partly performance by real actors, partly augmentation by effects. Burger's team built a set piece that stood in as the top of the Hancock building, and filmed Woodley (and other Dauntless) there, going down a short zip line. Later, Greg Baxter's effects team shot footage of the top of the tower from a helicopter and wove it together with a scene showing Tris on the ground after her ride. This scene was several months in the planning, as the producers needed to find a way to do it well while staying within the constraints of their budget. It's a short scene in the film, but important for establishing one of the high points of Tris's initiation into Dauntless.

Theo James (Four) and Shailene Woodley (Tris) balance in front of the green screen shooting one of Four's fear landscapes: the high wire.

Dauntless cast members set to catch Shailene Woodley (Tris) from the zip line.

OFF-CAMERA FUN

Weeks of training had bonded the cast, and they unwound after their workdays with evening trips to concerts and sporting events. Christian Madsen threw out the first pitch at a June Cubs game, and several cast members were on hand the night the Chicago Blackhawks beat the Los Angeles Kings to advance to the Stanley Cup finals. A group of actors also rocked out at a Rolling Stones concert, where surprise guest Taylor Swift joined Mick Jagger onstage.

Veronica Roth found that some of the most lighthearted moments were during on-camera rehearsals. "That's when they're still blocking the scene so everyone knows where to go," she says. "The actors go through the scene very

Above: Amy Newbold (Molly) and Ben LLoyd-Hughes (Will) at a Cubs baseball game in June 2013.

Below: Ben Lloyd-Hughes (Will), Christian Madsen (Al), and Amy Newbold (Molly) were the cast members who sang during the Seventh Inning Stretch.

quickly, and they usually have a little fun with it—Theo James and Shailene Woodley were frantically tapping on this green-screened computer one day, and I remember Theo saying, 'Quick! I have to update my Facebook status!' and Shailene responded, 'But what do I tweet?!'"

Actors Shailene Woodley and Zoë Kravitz continued to connect. Woodley says, "We have a lot in common. Before we met, we had mutual friends, so we already had a respect and a love for each other before we actually connected face-to-face, and it's been great to have her. We're surrounded—we have ten brothers in this movie, so it's nice to have a sister on your arm."

Their "brothers" bonded in a different way: by constantly joking around. Their humor reached its height (or its low point) after a visit from author Veronica Roth. As Miles Teller, who plays Peter, tells it, "There are a couple of characters in this movie that die, right? So I said 'Veronica, if you could bring one character back, who would it be?' She said, 'Oh, it would be Will. I always loved Will.' And so Ben [Lloyd-Hughes, who plays Will] was, you know, kind of happy and gloating or whatever." Teller thought he was just asking to be pranked.

So Teller asked one of the production assistants to buy a balloon and a card, which he put in Lloyd-Hughes's trailer with a note, supposedly from Roth, saying that the two should get together to talk about Will's role in future films. Lloyd-Hughes could text her, the note said. But the number on the card belonged to Jai Courtney, who played Eric.

"So Ben was telling us, 'Guys, I think Will's getting a spin-off. I think he's coming back from the dead. She didn't talk about resurrection, but that was the general vibe,'" Teller remembers. "I was laughing so hard. But then he was texting Veronica with Jai sitting next to him. And when he heard Jai's phone, he figured it out. . . ."

Lloyd-Hughes still laughs when he hears the story. "It was tragic," he says, shaking his head. "That's all I'm saying."

Shailene Woodley (Tris) and Ansel Elgort (Caleb) have fun between takes.

MEETING KATE WINSLET

While the **Dauntless** cast was together in Chicago from the beginning, other actors arrived only as their scenes were being filmed. The one who arrived last was the one they were most eager to meet.

Producer Lucy Fisher says, "There was kind of a mythical buildup to the arrival of Kate Winslet, who is admired and respected and a little bit feared by the rest of the cast. She arrived in character with six-inch heels, and she wore them the whole time, and at first she was a little purposely distant, I think. Just to show that Jeanine was not one to be tangled with."

Winslet was five months pregnant while shooting, but that didn't slow her down or soften her tone as Jeanine. In scene after scene, her frozen demeanor captured the camera and dominated the characters around her. Her performance was commanding and strong.

Lucy Fisher says, "I'd say that for us as producers one of the best moments was watching her arrive with her eight or ten wigs, and getting to figure out how she wanted to look. And we'd seen the Erudite costumes on Erudite people already, but never on an Erudite Oscar winner, marching in and taking charge. What she can do with a glance or a toss of her

Above: Jeanine Matthews (Kate Winslet) intimidates even the toughest members of Dauntless.

Right: Makeup artists prepare Kate Winslet's (Jeanine Matthews) hand for a big scene.

head, before she even speaks . . . it kind of knocks everybody around and raises everybody's game."

Winslet's schedule didn't allow her to stay on set as long as the other actors, but she regretted not spending more time with them. "I have just been here for a very intense three-week period," she said when it was over. "But these guys have all been at it for three months. And so, for me, it's been wonderful to get this concentrated chunk of time, but it's also been quite sad, because I've been slow to get involved with the fantastic rapport on set, this great camaraderie which is very much Neil Burger's doing. He crafted these relationships, very early on, with all of the actors."

Winslet saw a lot of herself in Shailene Woodley and made sure to encourage her through the long days of work. "She reminds me a lot of myself when I was twenty-one, you know," says Winslet. "You have to have a determination and a focus to be able to pull something off like she is. I remember feeling like that, feeling as though I had to be the one that led the troops on, and she very much has that spirit. I have absolutely been there, and it's like preparing for a marathon."

> "THERE WAS KIND OF A MYTHICAL BUILDUP TO THE ARRIVAL OF KATE WINSLET."
> —PRODUCER LUCY FISHER

"THE FIREWORKS OF WATCHING
A PREEMINENT ACTRESS OF HER
GENERATION UP AGAINST A PREEMINENT
ACTRESS OF THE NEW GENERATION . . .
WE JUST STAND AND WATCH IN WONDER."
—PRODUCER LUCY FISHER

DIVERGENT FANS IN THE HOUSE!

The reality of adapting a beloved book—such as *Divergent*—in the age of social media is that nothing is really secret. Although the filmmakers tried to keep production details confidential, it was inevitable that information would slip out in a project with so many people and moving parts. Soon it was all over *Divergent* fan sites that the film's working title was *Catbird*, and as observant fans saw Catbird signs crop up around Chicago, they posted the information on Facebook and Twitter. Before long, the fans had a rough idea of where the cast and crew would be in coming days. Some sets were completely closed to fans, of course, but some were right out in the open, like the Abnegation village. When the fans appeared there, the actors were generous with their time, welcoming visitors and taking photos with them whenever possible.

Left and above: Loyal *Divergent* fans pose with Shailene Woodley (Tris) and Theo James (Four).

In addition, the production made some large casting calls for extras in the Chicago area, to play nameless members of the different factions. Fans who fit the descriptions flocked to play, as one press release described them, "people with severe/fierce/intimidating appearance—athletic or bodybuilder a plus," or "people with a sweet disposition, hippie, mother-earth-type vibe or bohemian look—longer hair preferred (both men and women)."

Executive producer John Kelly says, "People want to know what we're doing. People want to know where we are shooting. They want to see the sets. They want to see what the actors are wearing. We've had them meet the actors, and they go crazy. And it's just so sincere that you're so excited about what this is going to be like when it's all said and done. We have to do the best job of making this book into a movie so all these fans go to see it again and again."

Rather than shutting out the fans, then, the film team invited them to spread the word that the film was capturing the spirit of the book . . . and more.

THE PERFECT CAMEO

As she was writing her first novel, Veronica Roth did not anticipate that someday there would be a film version of her book . . . or that someday she would appear as an extra in that film! But Roth was up for the challenge, and it drew her even more deeply into the process of making the film.

For this book, she participated in a brief Q and A about the experience.

WHAT ROLE DID YOU PLAY?

I am a Dauntless member who is about to go zip lining—in the scene, a group of us burst through a door, breathless, and look out over the city, and then zip lining starts and we all cheer on Tris as she goes.

WHERE DID YOU SHOOT THIS SCENE?

On a Cinespace soundstage! It was a fake Hancock building rooftop surrounded by green screen.

WHAT WAS IT LIKE?

For me, it was mostly . . . scary! I have never had any desire to do any acting—ever. I'm terrible at it and I'm very uncomfortable on camera, which is not the best combination for a movie cameo! So I had to summon some bravery that day. My job was to burst through the door first, then pause and look around with mixed breathlessness and wonder, then walk to a railing—and when we were shooting, I kept just making a beeline for the railing, basically running away from the camera. But everyone was incredibly kind and patient with me—Neil kept coming over to help me out, and Artist Robinson, one of the assistant directors, gave me a few pep talks. Eventually I think we got a take or two they could use, which is a relief! The best part of the day, though, was wearing the costumes and getting "tattooed" (I got one on my neck!), quite literally becoming a part of the movie I had, until that day, been watching from the sidelines. It was one of the last days of shooting, and scary and uncomfortable though it sometimes was, I wouldn't trade that experience for anything.

DID YOU HAVE ANY LINES?

It is with great relief that I tell you no. I did not have any lines.

Left: Author Veronica Roth appeared as a Dauntless faction member in the zip line scene.

Below: Dressed as Dauntless, author Veronica Roth shares a laugh with Shailene Woodley (Tris) and director Neil Burger.

WHAT KIND OF DIRECTION DID NEIL GIVE YOU?

He told me to focus on a single goal at a time—he suggested, in this case, that my "goal" after bursting through the door be "to catch my breath." He was trying to get me to shut out all my busy thoughts and focus on one thing at a time and make it genuine. It was great advice! But what I most appreciated about it was how calm and patient he was, even though I was clearly slowing filming down. It made me feel a lot more comfortable.

WHAT DID YOU WEAR?

I wore the standard Dauntless gear: black boots, black pants with mesh pockets (similar to the ones Shailene is wearing on the cover of *Entertainment Weekly*), a grayish-black sweater. The scene takes place after the Dauntless play Capture the Flag, so we were all wearing these grayish vests with little lights attached to them for the game. And, of course, my beautiful neck tattoo, and some Dauntless-style earrings made of nuts and bolts.

WHAT ELSE CAN YOU TELL ME ABOUT THE EXPERIENCE?

Being an extra is hard! It involves a lot of waiting, wearing heavy costumes in warm rooms, reacting to fake things on green screens, maintaining high levels of energy for long periods of time . . . and no one wants to be the one who screws up the take, so you have to focus. I'll never think of movie extras the same again!

Left: As an extra, author Veronica Roth looks on during the zip line scene.

Above and right: Author Veronica Roth's mother appears as an Erudite extra in the film. Seen here, above, with costume designer Carlo Poggioli and, right, in scene.

IT'S A WRAP!

Filming in Chicago finished in the middle of July 2013. Neil Burger still had many months ahead of him, cutting and editing the film, but the rest of the *Divergent* team was moving on to new projects until they came together again to promote the film. Kate Winslet was expecting a baby; Shailene Woodley was about to start filming *The Fault in Our Stars* (where Ansel Elgort, who played her brother in *Divergent*, would play her love interest); Veronica Roth was just months away from publishing *Allegiant*, the final book in the Divergent trilogy, which was certain to soar up bestseller lists. And the fans? Well, they still had a while to wait.

In the end, says producer Doug Wick, "*Divergent* is a movie about empowerment. It's set in a world that doesn't quite work and it basically says: If you can dig deep inside yourself and power through, you just might be okay."

And Tris Prior, indeed, is at once empowered and endangered as the story comes to a close. She thought she'd made the most important choice of her life at the Choosing Ceremony, choosing Dauntless over Abnegation and putting faction over blood. Now the consequences of her original choice are clear. Unintentionally, she helped make Abnegation vulnerable to the Erudite aggression. Now her family is ruined, the factions are in tatters, and her city is on the brink of revolution.

But Tris is full-fledged Dauntless now, as tough and brave as they come. She's better than Dauntless, in fact—she's Divergent.

From left to right: Producer Doug Wick, Ashley Judd (Natalie Prior), Shailene Woodley (Tris Prior), Ansel Elgort (Caleb Prior), Tony Goldwyn (Andrew Prior), and director Neil Burger enjoy time together on set with author Veronica Roth.

READ THE COMPLETE

DIVERGENT
SERIES

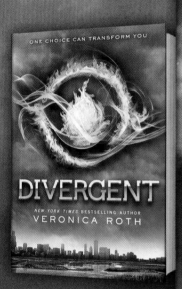

ONE CHOICE CAN TRANSFORM YOU

DIVERGENT
NEW YORK TIMES BESTSELLING AUTHOR
VERONICA ROTH

ONE CHOICE WILL DEFINE YOU

ALLEGIANT
#1 *NEW YORK TIMES* BESTSELLING AUTHOR
VERONICA ROTH

ONE CHOICE CAN DESTROY YOU

INSURGENT
#1 NEW YORK TIMES BESTSELLING AUTHOR OF DIVERGENT
VERONICA ROTH

BY #1 *NEW YORK TIMES* BESTSELLING AUTHOR
VERONICA ROTH

 /DIVERGENTSERIES
 KATHERINE TEGEN BOOKS
An Imprint of HarperCollins Publishers
DIVERGENTOFFICIAL.COM

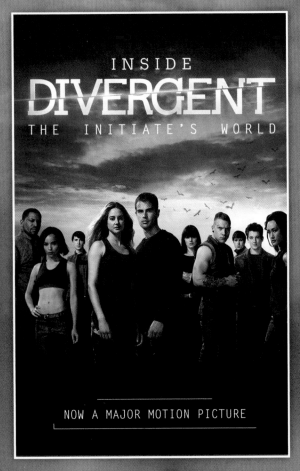
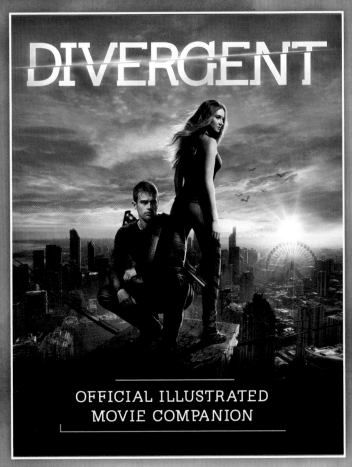